THE STORMS
OF DELIVERANCE

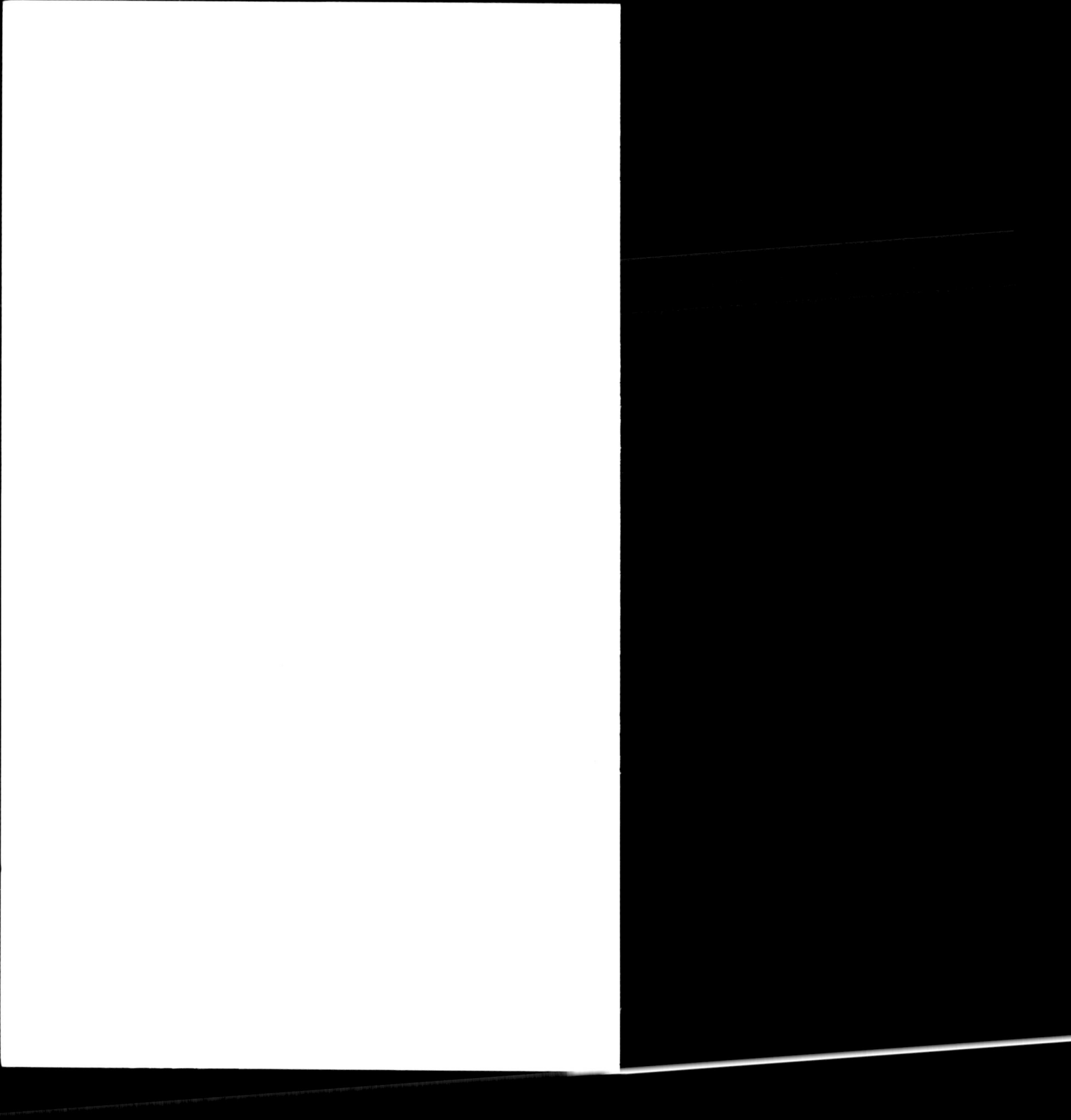

THE STORMS OF DELIVERANCE

A Novel

LARRY HIGDON

Tate Publishing & *Enterprises*

The Storms of Deliverance
Copyright © 2011 by Larry Higdon. All rights reserved.

No part of this publication may be reproduced, stored in a retrieval system or transmitted in any way by any means, electronic, mechanical, photocopy, recording or otherwise without the prior permission of the author except as provided by USA copyright law.

This novel is a work of fiction. Names, descriptions, entities, and incidents included in the story are products of the author's imagination. Any resemblance to actual persons, events, and entities is entirely coincidental.

The opinions expressed by the author are not necessarily those of Tate Publishing, LLC.

Published by Tate Publishing & Enterprises, LLC
127 E. Trade Center Terrace | Mustang, Oklahoma 73064 USA
1.888.361.9473 | www.tatepublishing.com

Tate Publishing is committed to excellence in the publishing industry. The company reflects the philosophy established by the founders, based on Psalm 68:11,
"The Lord gave the word and great was the company of those who published it."

Book design copyright © 2011 by Tate Publishing, LLC. All rights reserved.
Cover design by Kenna Davis
Interior design by Sarah Kirchen

Published in the United States of America

ISBN: 978-1-61346-529-5
1. Fiction / Psychological
2. Fiction / Sports
11.08.29

For all the children and animals
of the world.
And for my niece, Laura Cumbie,
an outstanding writer herself,
without whose help and encouragement
this novel would never have been written.

"The agony of overcoming personal limitations is
the agony of spiritual growth."
Joseph Campbell, *The Hero with a Thousand Faces*

CHAPTER 1

Johnson was in a terrible mood, and getting this kitten into a carrier in the middle of the night was making it worse by the second. He had to load the kitten from above, and every time he got her close to the carrier, she extended her legs out as inflexibly as two-by-fours so that she wouldn't fit. Plus she yowled as though someone were stepping on her tail. *She's going to wake up the kid,* he thought, *and it'll really be downhill from there.*

How does Manny get me into these things? he chastised himself. *How does he always get me to say yes? I told him I'm no good with little kids. "It'll be easy," he said. That's what he always says. Haven't I learned by now? I've known him for more than thirty years, and is anything ever as easy as Manny says?*

He wasn't thinking well. For starters, he had forgotten his wallet. He had almost arrived at Carrie's house when he realized that he had left it at home.

All he had been able to think about all day was Katy's letter. Katy's letter. *Why? Why did she write it? Where did I go wrong?* Less than a week ago she had spent the night at his apartment for the first time since their divorce. He remembered that she had left before he had awoken. *But if she had a problem, she would've stayed, right? Talked about it? That's what she does, isn't it? Talk about problems? She's a counselor, for God's sake! They talk about problems, or at least they call you, they don't just write a frickin' letter that doesn't make any sense!*

"Here," said Carrie. "Let me have Taffy. You get Rags out to the car."

"Mm," he grunted. Rags, the big, bouncing, white shaggy dog. I'm supposed to put this polar bear in the backseat of a 1968 Volkswagen Beetle. He put the leash on, but even at six-foot-two and with most of the muscles he had sported long ago as a baseball player, he found that Rags led and he followed, first to a shrub where Rags relieved himself, then in a roundabout romp to the car.

That's when he reckoned that he had made a serious strategic mistake. Ellen was already in the car seat in front. It wouldn't be possible to cram that dog in back without folding the front seat forward, which was sure to disturb the child's sleep. So he grabbed up the kid, laid her across his left shoulder, and dragged Rags back to the house.

But when he explained the predicament to Carrie, she replied, "Lee, you didn't have to do that. All you had to do was go around and put the dog in from the driver's side."

"Mm," he grunted, and back to the Beetle he trudged. He noticed that Carrie had accomplished the task of depositing Taffy into the pet-mobile, although he could still hear the cat yowling.

For no good reason he could think of, he glanced at the calendar just inside the front door to the house.

It was Tuesday, August 5, 2008.

Carrie took Ellen, whom Johnson was holding like a bag of oats. Rags again dragged Johnson all the way around the front yard, sniffing for the perfect shrub to use as a toilet, then hiked his leg before permitting Johnson to direct him to the car. "Okay," grumbled Johnson. "Just be sure you've taken care of business, mutt. I don't want to have to stop for you every fifteen minutes." The question occurred to him, how was he going to know when Rags needed to relieve himself? This pooch bounded about constantly, regardless of the circumstance.

By the time Johnson and Rags had returned to the car, Carrie was there, loading the cat carrier with its yowling feline, bowl of cat food, and litter pan onto the backseat. Rags followed enthusiastically. Ellen continued to sleep soundly in the front, her left thumb in her mouth, her straight, blonde, shoulder-length hair covering most of her face.

"Let me get her bags," said Carrie softly so as not to wake the child.

Johnson went to the front of the Beetle and opened the trunk. He had only half-packed his duffel bag, the navy blue one with the Braves' insignia that he had kept for almost twenty years, leaving plenty of space for the little girl's two cases.

As he was about to climb into the car, Carrie touched his arm, her chubby face looking up at him. "Lee, I have to ask you something."

"Yeah?"

"Have you had anything to drink today?"

He rolled his eyes. "No."

"All day? You mean you haven't had a single drink all day?"

"What do you want me—"

"Shhhh! Don't shout! You'll wake Ellen!"

Through clenched teeth he continued, "What do you want me to do, take a Breathalyzer? A blood test?"

"She's my granddaughter, Lee! I had to ask." She folded her hands across her ample abdomen. "Anyway, thank you for doing this."

Without answering, he got into the car. He had to slam the door three times to get it shut. He had tried to explain to Manny that this jalopy was in no condition for a two-hour drive to Augusta. Manny tended to ignore facts that he didn't like.

So off they went, cat whining, dog sniffing and licking, child still sleeping. *This kid would snooze through the bombing of Afghanistan,* thought Johnson. *That's one lucky break for me, anyway.*

CHAPTER 2

Leaning against the side of the car, a gas pump locked into its receptacle, he removed Katy's letter from his shirt pocket and read through it again under the lights of the BP station.

> Dear Johnson,
> I apologize for saying what I have to say in a letter rather than in person, but a letter gives me time to think about my words. I feel that this is such an important communication; I have to get it right.
>
> You know I love you, and I always will. Sometimes people grow apart, and I think that happened to us. You are not the same man I married in 1983; but let's face it, I'm not the same woman.
>
> Did you ever think in your wildest imagination back then that I would end up an elementary school counselor? That I, who didn't even want to have children when we first married, would have such passion for kids?
>
> Somewhere along the line I changed fundamentally. If the me now had been the me in the late 70s, you

never would have been interested in me. We never would have married in the first place.

Of course, we have other problems. Major problems. Number one, despite all my entreaties and all your promises, you continue to drink. Please don't try to deny it. I realize that you don't see your drinking as a problem. I can understand your point of view, but I disagree.

Johnson, you know I have a hard time with this because of my father. It's a very big deal with me. And the worst part is that you lied to me, which, for what it's worth, is what addicts commonly do. Trust is essential to a good relationship. Trust requires truth. If you would only admit that you have a serious problem and seek help! But I'm way beyond hoping that will ever happen.

A certain bond connected us when we met. We both grew up in miserable circumstances. It appears that one of us has been able to overcome the past and one of us has not.

Johnson, it would be so great if you would take a hard look at yourself in the mirror and take stock of your life. You're forty-eight years old. You may be too old for baseball, but you aren't too old to find an alternative to baseball that you could find enriching and rewarding. But I feel like I'm asking for an ambition or a drive that doesn't exist, never has and never will.

I have to conclude that our relationship doesn't work. I think it's better for both if us if we go our separate ways. I'm asking that you not call me again. Of course, we'll get together on special occasions for

Zoe. We'll say our "Hellos" and "How are yous," and that will be that. It has to be that way. We must end this relationship. I'm sorry. I'm hoping that after you read this, you'll understand.

Love forever,
Katy

He stuffed the letter back in his pocket. *Drinking. It always comes back to that, no matter how many times I tell her I can stop any time I want. I'm not an addict, she just refuses to believe me. I stopped smoking, didn't I? We both made a Y2K promise and we both kept it!*

As an aside, he wondered how she knew that he was still drinking. During the last several months, when they had been dating again, he had never drank alcohol in her presence.

Settled in his seat and ready to resume his trip, he decided he never wanted to see that stupid letter again. He rolled down the window, wadded up the letter, and tossed it into a nearby trashcan.

This maneuver turned out to be a mistake. Where barking dogs, yowling cats, human conversation, and Atlanta traffic had failed, the summer night breeze that wafted in through the window succeeded in waking Ellen.

"Where we going?"

"I'm taking you to your mom. And your grandpa."

"What about Daddy?"

"Him, too."

Rags leaned forward and licked his ear. Johnson pointed to the back seat with his thumb. "Do they fight?"

"No, they like to play. Mommy says he's sick, and I can't see him."

"Well, we'll let your mommy make that decision. But you're definitely going to see her and your grandpa." Her dad *was* sick in a way. That's how all this had gotten started. Lance had been admitted to the Veterans Administration's mental hospital in Augusta for treatment of his post-traumatic stress disorder from the Iraq war. Manny and his daughter Marla now realized that the treatment wasn't going to end for several weeks. The kid had been staying with Manny's ex Carrie, but now Carrie had to take a business trip to New York, and there they were. Somebody had to take Ellen to Augusta, and Manny had talked his good ole buddy into doing it.

He wondered if he should have suggested that Katy take the kid to Augusta. But he didn't know how well Katy even knew Ellen. Had Ellen ever been referred to Katy? Besides, he didn't want to call Katy after that letter.

Ellen's head was craned around to the right. "Look at all the lights!"

They had just turned onto Interstate 20, and had not yet left the city. It occurred to Johnson that Ellen had very seldom, if ever, seen the city at night. Streetlights bathed the highway in gold and turned bluish-gray streets to a golden brown. Though most were closed, many stores, restaurants, and theaters had their neon lights blazing into Ellen's wide-eyed gaze.

"There's red and green and blue and purple and red and orange and purple and yellow and…" As foul a mood as consumed him, Johnson almost smiled at the way her

Ls and Rs sounded like soft, round Ws, a fact that seemed heightened by her sleepiness. Her "orange" came out "arnge."

This recitation continued for quite a while before the lights became more and more sparse and she became bored with it. Ellen turned around to check the backseat. "Hi Rags. Hi Taffy."

Taffy remained curled up in the carrier directly behind Ellen, looking like an orange-and-white softball with a mouth that emitted loud meows. Ellen's words, however, sparked renewed excitement in Rags, who bounced around so hard that the shocks squeaked. *Fine*, thought Johnson, *I can just see us tipping over onto the shoulder because of Bigfoot back there.*

"Aw, Taffy, don't be sad," said Ellen. She turned to Johnson. "Taffy don't like riding in cars."

Johnson didn't respond. His steely gaze fixed on the road ahead, his mind still teeming over the letter.

"I'm five," she said.

"Mm-hmm."

"My next birthday I'll be six."

"Mm-hmm."

"Can we turn the radio on?" she asked.

"No, honey, I'm afraid not. It doesn't work."

"Can I try?" she reached for the button, straining as far as her seat belt would allow, and managed to punch it. What emanated from the dashboard was a loud buzzing static, no more pleasant a sound than a rusty chain saw. Johnson turned it off as Rags barked.

"See?" he said. He knew that it wasn't quite true that the radio didn't work. Problem was, it worked only if he held the driver's side door open about six inches. That was a maneuver he had no desire to attempt at sixty-five miles per hour with a hand into which his arthritis had spread.

"Are we gonna stop for ice cream? Mommy always stops for ice cream."

"I don't think any place is open, sweetheart."

She slumped in her seat in a pout as they proceeded in silence for a while. Then, "I need to pee-pee."

Rags slobbered on his ear again. Johnson began to imagine, given Manny's fat neck, how long it would take to strangle him. "Try to hold it, okay? I'll find a place."

"We can stop here. I can pee-pee in the grass."

Fortune smiled. A sign directed them to Doug's World Famous Donuts, open 24 hours, at the next exit, just two miles ahead. "Do you like doughnuts?"

Her eyes beamed. "Yeah! Are we gonna have doughnuts?"

"We sure are. And you can go pee-pee there."

"Can I have chocolate?"

"You sure can."

He wheeled into the parking lot, the only car there. He unbuckled her and held her hand as they walked up a steep incline to the store.

"Wait!" she said, looking over her shoulder. "We have to bring Rags an' Taffy!"

"They'll be fine in the car."

"No! They'll get too hot in the car!"

He kneeled down to look into her eyes. "No, they won't. It's not that hot now. And, see? I rolled down the back window a few inches. They'll feel the cool night air."

Once inside, he led her to the women's restroom. At the door, he asked, while praying for the right answer, "Do you need help?"

"No! I'm a big girl."

There is a God after all, he thought.

He treated her to a chocolate, cream-filled doughnut, which she would not eat until he got one exactly like it himself. He purchased a cup of coffee for himself and a bottle of orange juice for her.

For the next five miles, Johnson thought the doughnut had put her to sleep for the duration of the trip. But suddenly her right arm shot out and reached for the glove compartment. "What's in here?"

He felt certain she would never reach it from the car seat. He was wrong. Lurching forward with all her might, she managed to open the compartment. Out toppled a silver flask right into her lap.

"What's this?" she asked.

"Here, let me have that," he replied, gently prying the flask from her fingers.

"What's in there? Is it more juice?"

He rolled down his window and hurled it as far as he could with his left arm. Even to think of drinking its contents now made him sick.

"What was it?" she persisted.

"Dragon poison."

Ellen reflected on this answer. "But what if we run into dragons? You threw it away!"

"I checked my map. There are no dragons between here and where we're going."

Filled with sugar and chocolate, and secure from dragons, Ellen fell asleep. Even Rags fell quiet. Johnson wondered, *You mean he sleeps?* Taffy's meows had diminished to a guttural whine, barely audible above the rickety engine.

◆

Johnson almost wished Ellen had not gone to sleep or that some rabbit or passing horse trailer would provoke Rags to start barking. This was the dullest part of the trip. On the last ninety-nine miles, none of the exits offered any of the twenty-four-hour fast-food restaurants that one normally found in civilized places. Traffic diminished to nonexistence. He had no radio (even if he had, he couldn't have picked up any stations out here), and of course no CD player in this relic.

Another disadvantage of the silence was the unwanted time it gave him to think about the letter again. *Why a letter? Why didn't she call me? Talk to me? At least give me a chance to respond.* The coldness of a letter belied Katy's well-honed counseling skills that should have more than adequately strengthened her defenses against his weak verbal ability. He wasn't exactly a past champion of the debate team. He pondered what he should do, what he could do. Should he send a letter in return? Call her? Maybe she wouldn't answer. He hated voice mail. Nobody ever called him back when he left a voice message. Should he drive out to her school, catch her there? The front office would call her: "Ms. Nguyen, you have a visitor in the office." She'd probably think it was some child's parent or a Department of Family and Children Services worker. He could hide behind a potted plant until she entered the office.

And then embarrass her to death. No, if he pulled a stunt like that, she would surely never speak to him again.

It was all so frustrating. He couldn't approach any of her friends. They didn't know him. Katy had never gotten around to introducing him to any of the fine folks at Redrock Elementary School. Prior to now, he had never given that slight much thought. But why hadn't she? Had she been that ashamed of him all these years? Was she afraid he'd show up drunk? Was she afraid he'd bring Manny?

And what if he had met her friends at school? Surely they blamed him for every tear she had shed since she had met him. And, he supposed, with good cause. He blamed himself for each and every drop of salt water that flowed from those pretty I-want-to-smile Vietnamese eyes. He blamed himself. Bad News Johnson was a loser.

As the dark miles passed by his window, his depression deepened. Then he decided.

He *would* write her a letter. A letter she'd never forget. He'd spend a month composing it if that's what it took to get all the words right. He'd start thinking about it now to pass the time.

No, can't do that. What if I think of something really grand to say? I'd have to stop the car and try to find paper and pen to write it down. Otherwise, just like those dreams in which his eloquence wooed Katy into his loving arms, he'd forget it all. To remember, he might end up pulling the Beetle over to the shoulder every five minutes. Ellen would wake up. The dog would start barking again. The cops would think he was drunk. And he didn't think he had a pen or pencil in the car anyway.

But the idea lifted that black veil of despondence. He had an idea! He had something to work on that might brighten his heart.

For the first time all night he felt good. Even his car, whose endurance he had worried about for such a long trip, was cooing like a happy pigeon.

CHAPTER 3

The eighteen-wheeler roared past them in the left lane. It was traveling so fast that it created a draft that moved the Beetle a few feet closer to the shoulder.

The driver of the truck honked his horn, as loud as a foghorn, and held it down for a good five seconds. *Jeez,* thought Johnson, *is he trying to wake up everybody in Columbia County?* Rags barked, and the VW shook as he bounded around. Ellen, however, continued to snooze. He remembered that when Zoe had slept at that age, a blast of dynamite couldn't wake her.

Then Johnson saw headlights coming directly toward him. After that split second of frozen disorientation, he realized that this was some fool who was driving west in the eastbound lanes of the interstate, and who had been on a collision course with the massive truck until the truck's horn had caused the driver to veer into Johnson's lane. Now the crazy driver was heading straight for his little Beetle.

Johnson swerved the car toward the shoulder and out of the path of the onrushing headlights. He could hear the pulsating rhythm of his own heartbeat.

In the dark, it appeared to be a pick-up truck. Tires screeching, the truck clipped the rear portion of the Beetle and sent it into a spin.

Johnson saw beyond the shoulder. The grassy hill descended steeply into a ditch. With all his might, he fought to keep his car on the shoulder, but the right rear wheel slipped over the edge, and the Beetle tumbled over and over and over, down into the ditch and up the other side of it, continuing to roll, at times airborne, shedding bumpers and hubcaps, until coming to rest upright but with the windshield cracked, the hood and sides bent, and two tires blown out. The roof had caved in. Johnson felt as though he had been stuffed into a tin can.

He then lost consciousness, for how long he couldn't tell. He was snapped out of it by Ellen's bawling. Quickly he checked her. She was terrified but apparently unhurt. Those damn car-seats worked after all.

He himself felt pain all over. The now-twisted rear-view mirror showed an ugly lump on the right side of his forehead. A warm river of blood flowed down his left cheek and into the corner of his mouth. Was there a cut there? Or was it on top of his head?

Looking back, he saw the animals. They seemed unconscious, but he could not tell whether they were alive or dead.

"Ellen," he croaked, surprised by the weakness of his own voice. "It's going to be all right, sweetheart." But she was so scared as to be inconsolable. Her wailing was the worst sound he had ever heard.

Then he smelled the gasoline. *Oh my God,* he thought. *The fuel line may have ruptured. Any spark could cause a fire.* He had to get Ellen to safety, immediately.

He unbuckled the little girl, who was kicking and screaming. His fingers hurt, but they were not broken, it was only the arthritis. He fumbled at the belt for what seemed like thirty minutes but was closer to thirty seconds.

He had to get them out of the car. His door was dented and stuck, its lock jammed. He slammed his shoulder against it, but sharp pain shot through his side. Ignoring the pain in his left arm, he tried to roll his window down, and the handle gave way grudgingly. Despite his seat belt, his body had been banged around inside the cabin of the VW, adding pain to his arthritic knees and hands. His worst injuries from the crash seemed to be the right knee, the ribs on his left side, whatever had caused the scratch on his face, and a blinding headache.

Grunting, sweating, using every muscle in his body despite sharp and stabbing pains, his efforts to lower the window widely enough to get both himself and Ellen through nonetheless failed. He considered squeezing just her through the opening, then telling her to run. But would she? And where would she run to? The highway? No. That wasn't an option. He had to get them both out, but himself first. And fast. The odor of gasoline was growing stronger.

Finally, he leaned back, raised both feet, and kicked out the windshield, which was already fragile.

"Come on, baby," he said, encircling her with his right arm, and grabbing the top of the window with his throbbing left hand. He used his left arm for leverage to pull them through the window. "We're getting out of here."

He could feel the sharp glass fragments cutting his arm and right side as he struggled to climb over the dashboard and through. It was like trying to climb through a barbed wire fence. A higher volume scream from Ellen told him that he had rubbed her too close to one of the sides he had broken out and she had been cut somewhere. "Hang in there, kid," he whispered. With one last plunge, his upper body was out, he and Ellen rolled down the dented hood, and toppled to the ground.

Ellen was now on top of him, crying loudly, her whole face twisted into a mask of anguish. He felt sticky spots on her face and pajamas, and wondered if they were bloodstains. But running his hand across her face, he found no cuts or abrasions.

Most of his face was in high grass and warmed by blood. Blades of grass pushed into his nostrils. He felt so tired. He wanted just to lie there for a while. He was now experiencing so much pain that he couldn't determine which part of his body hurt the most. But he knew Ellen was hurting, also. And that engine could blow any second. They had to move.

He pushed himself up. Upright, he hoisted Ellen onto his right hip. He detected odors of sweat, dirt, hot rubber, gasoline, and urine. Ellen had wet herself.

He tried to make a mad dash for the highway. That effort didn't last long. After two steps, his right knee buckled, and he collapsed to the ground in agony. Ellen cried even louder.

So now it was mostly a crawl, dragging Ellen by the hand. She fought his grip, but he squeezed as hard as he could. Better to break her hand if that's what was required to get her to safety.

With his left hand digging into the ground, he climbed the hill next to the interstate. When he thought they were far enough away from the vehicle, he rolled over, rolling Ellen over with him. He sat up and sat the girl beside him. He felt as though he were trying to breathe underwater. He wanted to speak to her, comfort her, but he hadn't the breath to sound out the words.

His heart pounded rapidly and hard. Ellen's face was dusty, red, and stained by his blood, grass, and tears as she continued to cry.

Suddenly Ellen looked back at the smashed vehicle. "Where's Rags? Where's Taffy?"

His words wheezed out of him. "They're in the car. I'll get them. Don't worry."

"No!" she wailed. She ran down to the car, waving her arms. *"Rags! Taffy!"*

"*No!*" screamed Johnson. *"Ellen! Stop!"*

He wobbled to his feet and attempted to run after her, but stumbled immediately, his legs crumbling.

Ellen scrambled through the front window. The backseat burst into flames.

"Ellen!" Johnson screamed again.

No voice, human or animal, emanated from the Volkswagen. The only sound was that of the deathly lapping flames, yellow tinged with red, sharply pointed wicked fingers reaching out of the windshield and the small opening in the driver's side window. Johnson stood up again, and fell down again. *"Ellen! No! My God, no!"*

The engine exploded. What had before been a motor vehicle containing a little girl, a kitten, and a shaggy dog, was now but a huge, roaring ball of fire, like a portion of a fiery meteorite that had slammed into earth.

"Noooooooooo!"

CHAPTER 4

Johnson watched the fire silently from his perch at the top of the hill. He was far beyond tears. The tragic whine of sirens and the flashing red-and-blue lights barely registered in his consciousness, which came and went, playing tricks on his mind, making him wonder what was real and whether the worst had actually happened. But it had.

He felt himself being lifted up, a hand on each of his elbows. From across a canyon, he heard voices, a man and a woman. "Sir? Sir?" He was aware of his feet touching the ground as darkness invaded his vision. Emotional pain had numbed all physical pain.

He awoke once in the ambulance. There was some sort of clear plastic gizmo over his nose and mouth. Blurry faces watched from high above.

When the medics noticed that he was trying to speak, they lifted the plastic mask. "Call. McBroom." His voice was barely above a whisper. The medics had to lean very close. He gave them Manny McBroom's cell number. He wasn't sure he had it right, even though he had been calling that number for years. But he couldn't summon the energy to talk any more.

And then the darkness arrived again.

His last thought was: *They are all gone. Ellen is gone.*

◆

Johnson was hooked up to only one IV. A machine near his bed beeped softly. Manny was leaning back in a navy-and-green cloth print chair that fit him snugly. He had fallen asleep with a book in his lap. He jerked upright when he noticed that Johnson was awake.

"Swung you a private room," said Manny.

"Thanks," rasped Johnson. It was irrelevant to him.

"You wanna watch TV?"

TV was irrelevant, too. "No… no thanks."

"Braves 're on. Playin' the Giants."

The Braves and Giants were irrelevant.

Johnson cleared his throat. He spotted a pitcher of water on a table next to his bed. Signaling to Manny, he whispered, "Water?"

"Oh, sure, man." McBroom found two plastic cups and a straw near the pitcher and poured one cup full. Johnson took a sip, but could hardly lift his head. More water ended up on his chin than in his mouth.

"What happened, Manny?"

"How much do you remember?"

Johnson hesitated. "More than I wish I did." He looked away.

"It was some old geezer. Drunk. He was drivin' the wrong way on the interstate. And just to make sure he did every single thing wrong, he was doin' about ninety and drivin' on a suspended license. And it was his fifth DUI."

"Yeah… yeah. That son of a bitch."

"Lee, the police want to talk to you when you're able."

Johnson tried to roll more to his left, to face McBroom. "Not much I can tell them."

"Lee. There's somethin' I've gotta ask you."

Johnson looked at him. "No, Manny. I hadn't had anything to drink. I was stone-cold sober."

"I had to ask."

"I know."

"They say you had a concussion. Does your head hurt a lot?"

He didn't answer. He didn't care if his head or anything else hurt. A nurse's aide, a tiny young Filipino woman, entered the room to check his vitals. She fiddled with the IV bag above him and re-inserted the tube into his left wrist. Her search for a suitable vein was painful, but he barely noticed.

When the nurse's aide left, he asked, "How is Marla?"

McBroom looked down. He sighed deeply. "Not good."

"Does she blame me?"

"Right now she's so loaded up on Xanax, she might be blaming the tooth fairy."

"I tried to save her, Manny. I tried."

"I know you did, Lee."

But had he? Was he trying to convince himself that he had done all he could?

McBroom told him that Marla wanted to return to Atlanta immediately.

"I can't go yet," said Johnson.

Manny stammered, "Um, I know that. I don't think Marla… I mean, she knows it wasn't your fault, I explained all that, I tried to…"

"She doesn't want me in the car with her."

"I don't know. It's just tha—"

"I didn't take care of her child. She entrusted her child to me, and I didn't protect her."

"This wasn't your fault, Lee. You know that."

"No. I don't know that. I keep replaying the scene in my head. Over and over. Could I have done something different? Was there anything I could have done that I neglected to do? Bottom line is, I didn't keep that little girl safe from harm. That was my responsibility, and I didn't do it."

McBroom shifted his feet nervously. "You need to get some rest," he said. "Come on back to Atlanta whenever the docs say it's okay for you to travel again. I'll drive Marla back home tonight."

"Okay."

"She's in no shape to drive. I'm gonna need to take her car and drive her back." He reached into his right front jeans pocket, fumbled around, then withdrew a set of keys, which he set on the table next to the bed. "My Volvo's parked in the garage. I'm leavin' you the ticket, and I wrote the space number on it. After you get well, you can drive it to Atlanta and catch up with us. I'm gonna have to make all the arrangements, you know, and I've never done anything like this before, but I have to do it. It's a sure thing neither Lance nor Marla can. I called Carrie, but she's in so many meetings, I haven't been able to get through to her yet."

Johnson thought, *What arrangements? There can't be a funeral. Ellen had already been cremated. They can put on a memorial service of some kind when they're emotionally ready. Table that. They'll never be emotionally ready. I know I never will.*

Manny reached into the closet and withdrew a small bag. "I'm leavin' you some clothes. And there's a hundred dollars in the pants pocket."

"Your clothes?"

"Yeah, well, they'll be a little big on you."

Johnson thought, *They'll fit me like a circus tent.* But Manny had thought all of these details through, which touched Johnson in spite of his mood. After all, Manny wasn't the sharpest nail in the toolbox, and the poor guy was no doubt over his head trying to deal with a tragedy he could never have imagined.

"Get some sleep, buddy," were Manny's parting words.

◆

His arms folded across his chest as though he were in a casket (during sleep his body hadn't altered its position), he gazed up at the drab off-white ceiling, and pondered. *If I had just held onto her more tightly so that she couldn't run back.* He should have known, after their stop at the doughnut place, that she'd never leave without Rags and Taffy even though, for all he knew, they were already dead by that time.

Or, if he had ignored the pain in his knee and gone all out, surely he could have caught her and dragged her back to safety. Why wasn't he tougher? Hop on one damn leg if that's what it took. He should never, under no circumstances whatsoever, none, zilch, have let her run to the car.

And what could have sparked the fire anyway? He had known that that was a danger. He had smelled the gasoline. It could have been so many things. Somewhere, most likely metal had scraped against metal, shooting sparks. Possibly when Ellen had climbed in the window, the VW had leaned in a direction that caused sparks to interact with spilled gasoline. That was a good theory, as good as any. For what it was worth, it was irrelevant. She should never have been allowed to crawl into that vehicle.

Johnson wanted to die. *I saved myself,* he thought, *and nobody else. A loser like me walks away from it all, and a precious child, her whole entire life in front of her, is burned to death. Incinerated. She might have been a doctor, a lawyer, she might have discovered the cure for cancer. She undoubtedly would have brought joy into a multitude of lives. Yes,* thought Johnson, *I should have been the one to die. I deserve it.*

At some point in the midst of similar ruminations that morning, dreamless sleep had overtaken him. But his agitation dissolved his sleep within a few hours.

Katy. What would she think of him now? Topping all the complaints in her letter, he had proven himself incompetent and cowardly in a life-or-death emergency.

He felt restless. Never mind what the doctors said about keeping him hospitalized to observe his concussion. He wanted to go home. He hated hospitals.

Slipping out of bed, he glanced down the hospital corridor. Lots of nurses buzzed around their station, but no one was checking rooms. The clock on his wall said three-thirty. The nurses were changing shifts. If he were going to sneak out, no time offered a greater opportunity than the present.

He slipped on Manny's khaki shirt and jeans. Thankfully, the big guy had left a belt. Both he and Manny measured the same vertically, six-foot-two, but Manny's body stretched much farther horizontally. Manny's waist measured fifty-two inches, compared with Johnson's thirty-six inches. Johnson cinched up the belt to the last notch. He was making no fashion statement here, but he couldn't have cared less. He wanted to go home. The hospital aggravated his depression.

Once he had located Manny's station wagon, however, his plans changed. He had noticed storm clouds to the west. His black state of mind would make concentration on a 250-mile trip challenging enough; he didn't need to complicate the drive further by driving through a thunderstorm. In truth, he felt afraid of driving. When he closed his eyes, he could see that dark monster with two yellow eyes hurtling toward him. He could see the driver, an old man with scraggly gray hair, deep-set eyes, and a gray goatee.

But wait. That part couldn't be true. It had been just after midnight. How could he have seen the driver? He must have dreamed that part.

An overpowering thirst overtook him, and not a thirst for water or Coca-Cola or apple juice. He wanted Scotch and he wanted it now. He made a quick detour to a liquor store and purchased three bottles. He reckoned that this would alleviate his headache also, which was growing fiercer by the minute. Then he decided to search for a motel for the night. In the Deep South, most storms occurred in the late afternoon and evening. By tomorrow morning the weather should be clear.

CHAPTER 5

He stood outside the motel room and continued to study the western sky at dusk. Black clouds obscured the sun, but its dying rays illuminated the landscape around him with an eerie glow. *No,* he decided. *I'm not leaving now. There's paper and a pen inside. I'll start working on my letter to Katy.*

Of course, he thought, *maybe I shouldn't wimp out because of a summer storm. If I end up having another wreck and get myself killed, well, what of it? Isn't that what I deserve? Maybe maimed instead of killed. That would probably be fairer: live the rest of my life in a wheelchair, a head on top of lifeless body parts, having to stay in some filthy state institution forever, hopefully living to be a hundred in that condition. At first lots of people would visit, but gradually fewer and fewer, then finally nobody. Their lives would go on, while I looked at dreary walls all day, get myself wiped every day by some fat, mean old nurse's aide, or better yet by some weirdo who gets his jollies doing it. Yeah, that's more like what I deserve.*

I saved myself.

But he decided to go inside. He sat down at a desk, twirled the pen, and poured half a glass of Scotch. He got as far as "Dear Katy," then scratched it out, rewrote it and scratched it out again. The alcohol began to cause drowsiness. He decided to lie on the bed for a while to see if relaxation would generate the right words.

He turned on the radio above the bed, uncaring what kind of station it was. As it happened, it was a classical music station. What he heard, however, was beyond irritating. Some baritone, apparently German, was emitting guttural sounds as though he had eaten one too many sausages, accompanied by a sole tinkling piano. The host of the program introduced this excuse for a melody as a song by someone named Schubert. Johnson thought that he wouldn't play this groaning at the funeral of his worst enemy. He turned the radio off. Piling the pillows against the headboard, he laid back again.

He heard distant thunder. *Looks like the weather's heading my way,* he thought.

The sky had become dark. *That's not the storm, fool. It's nighttime.* The digital clock on the radio read 9:22. So it had to be the night. The sun set late this time of year, but not that late. He had dozed off.

Later, after falling asleep again, he noticed one empty bottle among the original three. He wondered, *Is it possible that I've already drunk an entire bottle?* He couldn't recall having drunk that much. He lifted up his letter, which still read only, "Dear Katy," his handwriting now blurred. From past experience, he would know how drunk he had become by the number of clocks he saw on the radio. Currently he saw two, and they both announced that it was a quarter until midnight.

He switched on the radio button beneath the double clock again, hoping for music to keep him awake so that he could finish the letter. As he turned the dial, however, all he found was static. *Must be the storm,* he thought. *Drat the luck.* The only station that came through clear was that wretched classical music station.

This time he didn't mind so much what he was hearing. The music had a lively beat. So he even turned up the volume.

It was Beethoven's Fifth Symphony. He recognized it because Zoe had played it endlessly when she was in high school. She had fallen in love with the piece in her music class. Or, she had fallen in love with her music teacher. That was before Oak County had discontinued music because it didn't improve test scores.

There was something about those repetitive four beats, "Dum-dum-dum-dum." Zoe had tried to explain to him what the four beats meant, but he had never cared. Settling his head deeper into his pillow, he closed his eyes. What did it matter? Right now it was irrelevant.

If only I had the guts to commit suicide, he thought. *Who the hell wants me alive now? Not Marla. Not Katy. Certainly not myself. What a gutless wonder I am. I saved myself.*

Now the rain was lashing the window. Thunder cracked so loudly that Johnson turned up the volume on the radio again, this time as loud as it would go. Lightning flashed almost without a break. The lamplight in his room flickered, and the music skipped a beat. *Jeez,* thought Johnson through his inebriated daze, *this is a good one.*

Between the cracking and booming of the thunder and the near-deafening volume of the music, Johnson barely heard the other sound, like a knocking against the door. *Has a tree limb blown against my room?* he wondered. When the knocking sound got louder, he theorized that some idiot must be out in the rain knocking on his door, probably wanting him to turn down the volume. Pulling himself dizzily to his feet, he thought, *Somebody's got to have some kind of serious problem with music.*

His bleary head sank back into the pillows as he listened to the last part of the first movement. The music was ever-building toward a grand conclusion. The beat gathered strength, drums hammering to add a sense of drama that merged with the darkness in his soul.

Something or someone continued to knock relentlessly at the door. Lightning flashed, thunder rolled, and the lights flickered again.

Finally he got up again and staggered closer to the door, the pounding leaving little doubt that this was more than a tree limb. Some crazy person was at the door. Should he even open it? *If somebody's loony enough to be outside in this, he's probably an axe murderer.* But as the knocking persisted, his curiosity overcame his reservations.

It was midnight.

And standing at the door was Ellen.

Bright, almost blinding light surrounded her, far more impressive that the lightning show in the sky. She was wearing a pink dress, decorated with a white bow at her waist affixed to a wide white silk belt. On her right shoulder sat Taffy, with her tail encircling her. Her left hand held a black leather leash, leading to a collar around the neck of Rags, who sat panting by her side. She smiled radiantly.

"Ellen!"

Johnson backed away from the door. *It can't be*, he thought. Ellen? Did he say her name or only think it? Swaying from the quantity of Scotch and the shock of what he was looking at, he tumbled backward onto the bed and passed out.

♦

At two o'clock the next afternoon, Johnson had almost recovered from his hangover. He sipped a cup of black coffee that the motel manager had graciously offered. Had he offered it out of the kindness of his heart, or because Johnson's red eyes betrayed his condition? In any event, Johnson would be driving soon, a good two and a half hours back to Atlanta.

He wished that he could have found a Bloody Mary. Small-town Georgia sucked. He had settled for a carbohydrate-laden pancake brunch and this large cup of strong coffee.

He climbed into Manny's Volvo, and headed into the blazing western sunshine. Since he didn't know whether to blame his headache on the hangover or the concussion, he decided to blame both.

CHAPTER 6

Katy Nguyen, her best friend Tameka Frame, and her daughter Zoe emerged among the throng of about fifty from the double wooden doors of the Second Baptist Church of Oak County. The memorial service for Ellen had just ended. Tameka pointed to a picnic bench to the right of the building.

"Can we take a break for a minute? I need to process."

Zoe, wiping moisture from her right eye, asked, "How long was that service? It seemed like forever."

Katy checked her wristwatch. "About two hours."

"Too long," said Tameka. "That's too long for that much sustained sadness."

"Who was the woman with McBroom?" asked Zoe, as they all sat down.

"That was Marla, Ellen's mother," replied Katy.

"If she feels as bad as she looks, they need to up her medication." Marla's face, already as long and thin as an El Greco creation, appeared even more gaunt than usual. Her eyes seemed to have receded into dark caverns, accentuating the contrast with her pale skin.

Katy couldn't help but mark the difference in Tameka's countenance. Her ebony skin glowed and her eyes shone bright beneath her bangs. But now Tameka wore her serious look, her brows creased and her lips pursed. "I feel guilty. I didn't really know Ellen. But I'm sure a lot of my class will have known her from last year. What are we going to do? Will the grief counselors be there Monday?"

"Yes. They'll set up in the media center."

"Is that where you'll be?"

"No, I'll stay in my office. First day of school, you know. We may have more crises than just Ellen."

"So what should I do? What should I say?"

"That's a good question. We've never had anything like this happen at Redrock before."

Tameka leaned across Katy to address Zoe, "What does our child psychology major think?"

Zoe looked pleased to have been asked. She towered over her diminutive mother, having inherited her height from her father. Her hand swept her long straight hair from her forehead, where it tended to cover one eye. "It's been two months of summer vacation, you know. That's a long time for a child. Kids who didn't know her well may not even be thinking about her when school starts back."

"Good point," noted Katy, which made Zoe beam even more.

"So should I ask my class Monday if any of them knew Ellen? Or maybe make some kind of general announcement? Do you think the principal will make an announcement?"

"Mrs. Drummond sent letters out to all parents."

"Really? That was fast."

"You know Mrs. Drummond. 'Mrs. Hands-on.'" Katy was not a fan of the principal, who wanted her counselor to limit her efforts to helping kids raise their test scores.

"I don't know," said Zoe. "I wouldn't do that. I think you should keep a watch out for kids who seem to be sad or withdrawn."

Katy added, "Yeah, and make sure they're sad or withdrawn because of Ellen and not because it's just the first day of school."

"Right," said Tameka.

"If you need me to, I can come and talk to your whole class. We just want to avoid setting off a wave of sadness ourselves. Sometimes it's better to let the children come to us."

Tameka exhaled, her facial features relaxing. "Okay. Man, I've never begun a school year with more dread. I'll keep my eyes and ears open."

Katy handed Zoe the keys to her Prius. "Honey, can you bring the car around?"

She knew her daughter enjoyed driving it. "Sure, Mom. Be right back."

As she watched Zoe leave, Tameka observed, "Your little girl has grown up to be a Duke student. I never would have imagined it. No offense."

Katy smiled. "None taken. She can still be a teenager. She still has the requisite number of rings and tattoos."

"Well, you know, at least some part of her is her father's daughter, too."

A cloud of despondence moved over Katy's countenance. "I'm glad you mentioned him. I need to ask your opinion about something."

"Sure."

"I don't know whether to call him or not."

"Why in the name of heaven would that be a hard question to answer?"

"He's a jerk, Tameka, but he's been through hell. Manny told me about the accident. It was horrible. Can you imagine watching a child burn to death? Even Johnson would have to have a hard time dealing with that."

"And that's your problem why?"

"I just feel guilty."

"You feel guilty? After all he's put you through? Girl!"

"I wrote him this letter—you know, after I found the booze in his apartment. I know he must have been upset when he read it. He really wanted us to get back together."

"Mm-hmm. Wanted it bad enough to have lied to you for eight months. Just like he lied to you for those twenty-something years you were married."

"But what if he was so upset about the letter that it distracted him? So that he didn't react fast enough when that other car came toward him?"

"You mean what if the whole thing was your fault? Please don't tell me you're thinking that!"

Katy entwined her fingers and gazed down at them. "I don't know what to think."

Tameka glanced at her wristwatch. She shook her head and stood up. "I've got to go. But look. Before I met Gerald I got married when I was eighteen. The guy was a total loser, and it only lasted six months. But for two years after that, he kept bugging me to get back together. But whenever I went out with him, he treated me as awfully as ever. I think guys just get tired of doing their own laundry."

As she left, Katy heard her muttering, "Bad News Johnson!" Katy stretched back on the bench. Zoe should have been here by now, but that was Zoe. She had probably encountered friends along the way, started chatting with them, and lost track of time.

Yes, Johnson had lied to her. Again. Why did he have to keep messing things up that way? She thought back to their date the previous December. It had been the first time they had gotten together since their separation three years before.

CHAPTER 7

They had agreed to meet at the Ivy downtown. As Katy entered, Johnson waved from a booth by the window. Katy took off her plaid scarf and sat across from him. Shivering, she kept on her wool overcoat. Back in the day, they had insisted on sharing the same bench. That had been prior to many disagreements and hardships.

"I ordered you a hot chocolate. Hope that's still right."

"Right as rain. Or should I say 'sleet.' Think we'll be able to get home tonight?"

"If we can't, we're surrounded by hotels."

"Mm-hmm. The two-hundred-dollar-a-night kind. In case you've forgotten, I live on a teacher's salary. And you... what exactly do you live on these days?"

"We can sneak in and sleep on the couches if we have to. That could be fun, actually."

"You didn't answer my question."

"You assume I don't have a job."

"It was just a question," she said, holding her palms up.

"I'm working at Clyde's again. Money's not great. But in about four more months I have a chance to move up to assistant manager."

"You decided not to go back to school?" *Again?* she thought.

"Not just yet, no."

A waitress appeared, a young redhead wearing a Santa cap with white fringe and a fluffy white ball on top. In the background an orchestral version of "Good King Wenceslas" played, which happened to be Katy's favorite Christmas carol. *Could Johnson have somehow arranged that? No, surely just coincidence.* The carol blended discordantly among sounds of the low hum of conversation, the clinking of glasses and plates, and a waitress shouting at the bartender, "Gin and tonic, Bud Light."

"Have y'all decided what you want to eat?" The waitress set down a cup of coffee in front of Johnson and a hot chocolate for Katy.

"Tell you the truth, the lady hasn't had time to look over the menu yet. Just give us a couple of minutes, okay?"

"No problem. I'll be back in a little. Name's Candi." She pointed to the white nametag above her ample right breast. "If you need me, just holler."

Katy smoothed the napkin in her lap, then turned piercing eyes across the table to Johnson. "I thought you were going back to school this fall. You know, to study computers?"

"Oh yeah, that. I decided to put that off."

"Why? I mean, you seemed excited about starting a new career." *For once,* she thought.

"I wasn't sure computers was what I wanted. This job at Clyde's Closeouts, I'm in the computer section. Kinda gives me an idea about whether I'd really like computers for a living, you know?"

"But don't you have to have some expertise to sell them?" She sipped her hot chocolate and felt the warmth begin to thaw her bones, and the happy drug that chocolate supposedly contained lift her spirits.

"We need to look at the menu," he said.

"Okay." As she unfolded the menu, she began to wonder how much of his story she could believe.

The menu was bright blue, with depictions of food entrees. *Sugar, fat, carbs,* thought Katy. She was fighting hard these days to prevent her seasonal depression from leading her to gorging on food. She was going to have to see her psychiatrist about temporarily increasing the dosage on her anti-depressant.

She had heard someone (Manny? Johnson?) say that Johnson was on meds now also. As she sat across from him, she watched for signs of any positive change in him. So far she hadn't noticed any.

"I'll have the pasta salad," she said.

Johnson winked at the waitress, who returned to take his order for the Boomer Burger and her pasta salad. Katy thought the wink was flirtatious. That had been one of many underlying issues for her during her marriage to Johnson. He seemed to have a wandering eye. It made her feel embarrassed when she was with him. He denied it, of course.

"So," said Katy. "Why did you want to see me?"

"Getting right to the point, huh?"

"Why not?"

"You got a plane to catch?"

No, she thought. *No sign of change.* "Come on, Johnson. I'm just curious."

"I haven't been happy, babe," he said, his voice softer and deeper, as though self-conscious of the patrons sitting nearby.

"Oh?"

"When we agreed to the divorce, you know, my drinking had become, um…"

"Excessive."

"Yeah. You're right. And you know, it does something to your brain."

"Pickles it." She smiled thinly.

"I wasn't thinking clearly. Now that I'm not drinking, you know, as much, I feel like my mind cleaned house of all the crazy thoughts I was having."

"What crazy thoughts?"

"I said a lot of stuff I didn't mean. It was the booze talking."

"Maybe alcohol just removes inhibitions. So you say things you want to say, but you'd be afraid to say them unless you were drunk." She knew that her analysis was closer to the truth. *It may exaggerate,* she thought, *but it does not create. It can cause brain damage that results in hallucinations, but it doesn't create ideas.*

"Katy, I don't really believe that you're conceited, or that you look down your nose at me, or that you're ashamed to be with me because I'm not as educated as you are. That's not what I think. Not at all!"

He had said all these things during their marriage. She leaned forward, propping her elbows on the table and interlocking her fingers. "But you haven't stopped drinking."

"No… no. I'll admit that. But I've cut way back."

"So how much do you drink now?"

"How much?"

"How much. Like if it's beer, how many bottles per week? Or if it's Scotch—"

"I drink Scotch mostly, like always. But not much, really."

"So how many glasses per week?"

"Oh, I dunno. It's hard to say," he replied lamely.

"So many you've lost count?"

"No! Of course not! I'd say maybe two or three glasses, I guess."

She sat back against the light brown plastic cushion and gazed at him cynically. Did he think she could no longer tell when he was lying? After almost thirty years? "Johnson. You know how I feel about the alcohol problem."

"I know, I know," he said, waving off the topic. "What am I going to have to do, get a notarized statement?"

She stared out the window. It had stopped sleeting, but the slim coat of ice produced an enhanced contrast between the dark of night and the city lights, which seemed to have cold, golden auras around them. She felt a similar curtain of ice descending between them.

"Look, Katy—"

"I never know whether I can trust what you say," she said.

"Here you go," said the waitress, placing their orders in front of them. Then to Johnson, "You made short work of that coffee, huh? I'll get you some more."

"I'd like another hot chocolate," said Katy, speaking to the side of the waitress's head.

"Oh. Sure," said Candi.

After she had gone, Johnson asked, "You're not seeing somebody, are you?" Again his voice became soft and low.

Startled, she replied, "Where did that come from?"

"I dunno, it's just you seem so reluctant for us to spend time together, or maybe to get back together, or—"

"Johnson, I have plenty of reasons to be reluctant, as you well know. And, no, I'm not seeing anyone."

Both began to eat. "How's your salad?" asked Johnson with a mouthful of Boomer Burger.

"Good. So have you been dating?"

"Me? No! No!" He shook his head sharply.

She wiped her mouth with her large white cloth napkin. "It's like this. I just wish you would stop drinking. For good. And go to school and make something of yourself. And look at yourself in the mirror. And once and for all, accept that you did not become a major league pitcher."

He frowned. "That's not fair. I've accepted that."

"Then why is it that all you do is drink and gamble and lie about until you find another dead-end job like Clyde's Closeouts?"

"Always gotta harp about the drinking. Can't you ever give it up? I can handle drinking. It's not a problem like you always make it out to be."

"You think so. But I know how tricky alcohol can be. You think you don't need it, but the need sneaks up on you, and before you know it—"

"I'm not your father, you know. We've been down that road a million times."

"Denial. Not telling the truth. Those are clear warning signals of addiction."

"Well, I'm not an addict! That is the truth!" He crammed in another mouthful of burger.

She picked at her salad. "You know how it was."

"Mm-hmm. But it wasn't always like that. We've got a lot of years invested in us, babe. I'd like to think it's still possible for us to be good again."

But she found his pleading brown eyes no longer so hard to resist. "We had some very bad times, Johnson. Very bad. I can't just snap my fingers and make those kinds of memories disappear. And for that matter, neither can you."

"So we make new memories. Good ones."

"And how do we go about that?"

"We start spending time together again. Come home with me tonight."

Her eyes cut away. "Not a chance."

"Okay. Okay. Then let's meet like this for coffee or dinner or drinks."

"Drinks?"

"You'd be able to see for yourself that I can handle it."

"Mm."

Katy sensed a silence descend upon the table as though frozen fog had snuck into Ivy's Café and had settled on their table between them.

"So what do you say, babe?"

"I need to think about it, Johnson." What she needed to think about was their daughter, who wanted them at least to be friendly.

"Fair enough. I understand. I've been a first-rate bastard. Can I call you next week?"

"Yeah. Do that," she said in a voice so weak as to be almost indiscernible.

When they had finished their dinner and Johnson had paid the bill, they said their good-byes outside the café.

"Did you drive down?" asked Johnson.

"I took the train."

"I'll give you a ride."

Her half-smile reappeared. "You don't need to do that."

"I don't like the MARTA station this time of night. Too many weirdos."

"I know. I want to take a cab back to my car."

"Jeez, Katy. That'll cost you thirty dollars!"

"I can afford it."

"Okay… well… good night. I'll call you next week."

Their eyes met. He tried to hug her. Long ago she might have melted into him. Now she kept her distance. For her the feeling for him was genuinely gone.

The story of our marriage, Katy mused. *I became the level-headed one who's always sensible. He's the handsome ne'er-do-well I constantly have to forgive. All I did was marry my father. The power differential was forever off-kilter, or it was co-dependency, whatever. It was wrong.*

Numerous cabs were parked in front of the restaurant, some yellow, some white. She climbed into one with a Latino-sounding name that she barely glanced at.

As the cab pulled away, she looked back. She saw him walk across the street, and wondered whether he was headed for that strip club, The Tiger's Tail. *Maybe he parked his car in that direction,* she hoped.

⬥

She felt no enthusiasm for dating him again. Every time they met, however, he refrained from drinking any alcoholic beverage. He behaved like a perfect gentleman. She thought his medication might be helping him.

Then a couple of weeks ago, she agreed to spend the night at his apartment. Awakening with a fierce headache, finding no aspirin in his medicine cabinet, she searched through his kitchen. She found no aspirin, Advil, or Tylenol, but did find half a dozen bottles of Scotch, one of which was almost empty.

Her headache no longer seemed important.

⬥

She spotted her light blue Prius turning the corner and parking in front of the church. She walked slowly down the hill from the church.

As nervous as she was about the demands of the first week of school, she nonetheless looked forward to it. Working with children provided her therapy; the school provided her refuge. *I lost my heart to Bad News Johnson*, she thought. *I found it in the children.*

CHAPTER 8

Johnson awoke slowly, his left cheek pressed comfortably against the beige leather. He began to stand up but bumped his head on a cloth ceiling. He was no longer in their apartment. This wasn't the loose green throw that covered their couch. This was an automobile. Once his eyes focused on this apparent reality, he recoiled, throwing himself out of the vehicle and onto the dusty shoulder of an interstate highway.

What is this? he wondered. *What am I doing in this Volvo? Where's my Pinto station wagon? Where's our apartment? Where's Katy?* Turning slowly, he stared in every direction.

It was twilight, and the air was heavy and hot. His surroundings looked different, but vaguely familiar, as though a painting had been painted over in such a way that several important details were not the same. *It looks like Atlanta,* he thought. He had grown up in Atlanta. *But what would I be doing in Atlanta?*

The questions raced through his mind over and over. *Why am I here? How did I get here?* He had no answers.

And what's with these clothes? Instead of the long-sleeve blue shirt crisscrossed with yellow lines that he was supposed to be wearing, a gigantic khaki shirt swallowed his torso. His jeans, barely trussed up with a belt, were broad enough to fit four legs instead of two.

He started pacing. His head ached, mainly above each ear. His left ribs hurt enough to slow his breath, and every joint ached, especially his right elbow—that one he expected—and both knees.

What's the last thing I remember? Mental images seemed hidden in mist. Was this amnesia? *No,* he thought. He knew his name (Johnson), age (twenty-one), and address fully well. He knew who the President was (Reagan), knew the year (1981) and month (July) and day (the fourth); that is, unless he had lost some days while he had been asleep—or unconscious.

So it's not amnesia, he thought. *Where exactly was I when I fell asleep?* He concentrated. He had been sitting on a sofa, watching a NASCAR race on TV, drinking beer, dozing in and out of sleep. And he had been in Buffalo. Buffalo! Had he drank so many beers that he had blacked out and somehow journeyed all the way to Atlanta?

He observed the steady flow of vehicles along the highway. There was a mammoth truck transporting cargo for an outfit called Griswold's. It was the longest truck he had ever seen, longer than a boxcar. He saw lots of pickup trucks: fancy, humongous shiny creations with four seats.

Well, I'm sure I'm in the South. No other place would have this many pickups. He spotted a number of trucks that were larger than station wagons and completely covered. They were all over the place. And he saw so many small cars, many of which struck him as downright ugly. Nothing on the road looked remotely like his Pinto station wagon. He had to admit, however, that this Volvo station wagon, wherever it had come from, appeared a lot more comfortable than his Pinto. Not that that was saying much.

I can't just stand here, he thought. *Wherever this is, it certainly isn't Buffalo, if for no other reason than the heat.* Perspiration bubbled up on his forehead and rivulets rolled down his nose. *So I've got to get back there. I'll try to get back to Buffalo. And I'll keep hoping that somehow this is a dream.*

He noticed a large green sign with white lettering, but he couldn't read it from where he was standing. He climbed into the driver's seat and eased out onto the freeway, which was far from deserted, but neither was it locked in a stranglehold. There were too many lanes. Small rocks splattered and dust kicked up as his tires left the shoulder. As he approached the sign, he was relieved to find familiarity in what it said:

Indian Trail–Lilburn Rd
1 Mile

That street belonged to metro Atlanta, as he recalled. So now he was fairly certain that he was in suburban Atlanta, at least to the extent that he could feel fairly certain about anything. The sun, barely high enough in the sky to reach over the downtown buildings in the distance and flood the highway with burning yellow light, was over his left shoulder. That signified that he was traveling northeast. This could be I-85 North. If so, he could take Indian Trail to Lawrenceville Highway. At that intersection, he should find the apartment complex where he had once shared an apartment with his best friend, Manny "Mad Man" McBroom. If Manny was there, he would know what to do. Maybe.

The ride was scary. Indian Trail also had too many lanes. When had they added all these lanes? The unfamiliarity forced him to focus on driving and to minimize sightseeing and to try to ignore the pain, which included that pounding headache and aches in every body part.

But disconcerting sights abounded all around. So many apartment complexes. So many condominiums. Shopping centers and strip malls where they didn't belong.

The sign on his right announced Highway 29, Lawrenceville Highway, next intersection. He looked to his right. No apartment complex. Of course not, not any more than there was a rodeo. Another line of stores, selling tires and guns and booze like any good Southern stores had replaced the structures on this part of the road. *So what did I expect?* he thought. *Did I truly think my old apartment would be where it's supposed to be when hardly anything else is?*

He stopped at the red light at the intersection, contemplating his next move, distracted by the black monstrosity of a vehicle in front of him. *What on earth is that thing?* he wondered. It said "Hummer" on the back. He could not see around it or over it. He could barely see the traffic light. "It's like being behind an aircraft carrier," he grumbled.

He decided to turn left onto Lawrenceville Highway. There he discovered yet another surprise. Expecting a two-lane street—his side going east, and the other side going west—he instead found five lanes, including a middle lane set apart by a yellow stripe on each side for making left turns. As he progressed eastward, he saw yet more development—apartments, condominiums, and more strip malls, primarily filled with car repair shops—where previously there had been only single-family homes in yards overgrown with trees and kudzu. He saw sleek service stations, combined with little snack stores, showing ridiculous prices for gasoline. What he wasn't seeing were pay phones. He needed to find one to call Katy in Buffalo and let her know what had happened to him. He felt his heart rate quicken, and his breath grow shorter. In spite of the car's air conditioning, he was perspiring and even dizzy. The summer heat wasn't causing this. And the pain wouldn't abate.

He reached into his shirt pocket for the Valium that he normally kept there. Nothing. He decided to search for it in the glove box. With his shaking left arm holding the steering wheel, he opened the glove compartment and groped around inside. His right hand clasped around what felt like a prescription bottle. The bottle, difficult to read, bore his name and read—he had to hold it close—"Clonazepam." He had no idea what this was. Frustrated, he tossed the bottle on the passenger-side floor and slammed the glove box closed.

Why was the writing on the bottle so difficult to read? He realized that his vision must have deteriorated. Letters on the bottle and letters on signs blurred. *Was this where term "blind panic" came from?* he wondered.

Another jolt caused him to wheel into the next service station on his right. He took a long look into his rearview mirror. Yikes! His curly dark hair had thinned! He hadn't balded, but his hairline had receded, and his hair had turned silver on each side. He saw bags under his eyes and lines around the corners of his mouth. His forehead sported a bluish bruise on the right side, and the thin red line of a scratch marred his left cheek.

He felt impelled to run screaming out of the car. But he managed to keep a lid on his panic when he spotted a black box on a pole with the white design of a telephone on its side. A pay phone!

Do I have the change? he wondered. The phone demanded more than he had anticipated. Reaching into his left jeans pocket, he pulled out a bounty of bills. He counted a hundred dollars. A hundred dollars! What was he doing carrying that kind of cash around? Was he a drug dealer now? He got change from inside the service station, inserted the coins with fumbling fingers, and dialed the number to the Buffalo apartment.

The phone beeped. A mechanical female voice said, "We're sorry. The number you have reached is no longer in service."

Dizzy again, he leaned against the phone box. He tried the number for Chungking Charlie's, where McBroom worked, but met with the same result.

He had never felt more like having a drink. His vision had cleared, but the dizziness and headache remained.

Come-and-go blurry eyesight and a constant headache. What did that mean?

He returned to the car, intending to search for a bar. No Katy. No Manny. Fear and despair were rising far beyond his ability to cope with them. His mind worked better after a few drinks. Best antidote for pain in the world, too.

Right now, however, his hands were shaking too much to attempt driving. He withdrew his wallet. The old man in the driver's license picture stared back at him eerily. The address read "1768 Champion Circle, Duluth, Georgia." Fine. He remembered that Duluth was a northeastern suburb of Atlanta, but he had never heard of such a street.

After leaning against the car to gather his strength, he ambled into the snack store to purchase a map. What he came out with was easily an inch thick. Encyclopedia Atlanta. Just outside the door was an olive green box containing newspapers. He happened to glance at the issue on top of the stack inside the box. Its date: August 7, 2008.

He almost fainted. He ran back to the station wagon in such a frenzy that he ignored the shrieking pain in his joints. His stomach turned upside down. He threw up behind the vehicle again and again.

The year was 2008! How could it possibly be 2008?

Who am I, Rip van Winkle? No. No, of course not, that was not possible. He couldn't have slept along the side of a major interstate for almost thirty years without being rousted by a cop. No. This wasn't a van Winkle experience. It was something, had to be something, equally as bizarre. He had either traveled twenty-seven years into the future… or he was crazy.

If that was his choice, he preferred the former. He had somehow leapt forward in time. He was a time traveler. His last memory was of the summer of 1981. In Buffalo. With Katy. Watching television. *Did I black out?* he wondered again. He drank enough to suffer blackouts. But no. No blackout lasted twenty-seven years.

He recalled that Atlanta had been very hot in the summertime. But not like this. It was much hotter this afternoon than he had ever recalled in Atlanta, hot enough to stifle breath. Maybe hot enough to singe exposed skin if you were outside too long, like the opposite of frostbite. Even though a wind blew from the west, it felt like a blast furnace. The sky, as sundown approached, was so hazy that he couldn't tell whether clouds were up there or not. His shirt clung to his steamy, wet back.

So time travel, nutty as it sounded, had to be the answer. That was it. He had found himself in a different car in a different Atlanta in a year far into the future. He was in a new world. He was a much older Wilbur Leroy Johnson, and the year was 2008.

What can I do, he thought. *Where can I go? I have no idea where Lee Johnson, 2008 version, belongs.* Tears began to stream down his cheeks.

Suddenly his blood stirred, and his heart rate quickened. Somewhere in the car, somewhere in his wallet, there could be a name, a number, that he would find familiar. He would call anybody at this point. He pulled open the glove compartment, his hand raking out all the contents, some making it to the passenger seat, others falling to the floor. There was an insurance policy and a car registration card, both confirming that one Manfred J. McBroom owned this vehicle, or to be strictly correct, was paying Happy Bob's Finance Corporation for the privilege of driving it. Happy Bob's? Jesus! So what was he doing driving Manny's car? But he breathed a sigh of deep relief. His connection with Manny still existed. Wherever Manny lived now, that was good news.

Next he withdrew his dark brown wallet again, the color worn to white around the fringes, from his right back pocket. He leafed through photographs, an old one of himself and Katy standing in a close pose, another of his friend McBroom with a little girl with long blonde hair whom he didn't recognize. Could she be his? McBroom's previously red hair was white, and his physique was enormous in the picture. Then his breath caught as he viewed another photo of Katy, this one clearly an older Katy with telltale age lines around her narrow eyes and wide mouth. Besides that, she looked as spectacular as ever. Well, the great news was that they might still be together, wherever the hell they were together.

He stuck a finger behind the pictures and out poured a dozen or more cards and folded pieces of paper. Sorting through them, he discovered a card for A-Alpha Motor Club, another for Ralph's Towing, another… could this be right? Alcoholics Anonymous? *You've got to be kidding*, he thought. He needed some clue that could lead him to his home address or to Katy or McBroom. He found nothing like that. *Well, I haven't changed too much in thirty years,* he thought. *Never kept much of anything in my wallet.* The two folded sheets of paper each contained a woman's first name. Zodiac was one, Tigress the other. Sounded like strippers. There had been some attempt to record phone numbers, but they had been written by a drunk, and what difference would it make even if he could decipher them?

But maybe… maybe he didn't want to go "home," whatever that meant, just now. Maybe he didn't feel ready for whatever he might find there. Or whom. Maybe he should buy an airline ticket and fly back to Buffalo, where he could begin searching for Katy. But what if she were married now? To someone other than him? How would he handle that? He had long since passed his capacity for coping with disquieting surprises. He sat with his hands propped on top of the steering wheel for a time… how long? He didn't know. He only noticed that the sky had darkened. He decided just to drive, destination nowhere, like pacing on wheels, to try to clear his mind. He set off further east on Lawrenceville Highway. He would simply drive around for a while with the air conditioner on so that he could cool off, then maybe check into a motel for the night, and plot his next move.

◆

He drove as the streetlights flicked on and shadows cast by them began to appear. He drove as dark two-lane roads turned golden in his headlights. He drove slowly, true to form for a driver who does not know where he is going. Occasionally he would see headlights blaring into his rear view mirror, angry people who wanted him to go faster. Bullies behind wheels, who sought to intimidate by pressing close onto his rear bumper. Johnson noticed that these part-truck, part-station wagon creatures came equipped with extremely bright headlights. When their boorish behavior interfered with his attempt to relax, he would simply pull over to the side of the road, turn on his emergency lights, and let them pass.

Eventually he noticed a rather simple sign made of two gray slats connected by two other horizontal gray boards. The sign read "Fraser Park" in yellow lettering. He pulled in and parked near the entrance. He walked down a narrow lane beneath overhanging trees on both sides. The vegetation was so lush it created the impression that any city was far away. Or was it intended to remind the visitor of the Garden of Eden? Or was it in fact the Garden of Eden? Had he tripped his way through time again? Lee Johnson walked over the ages like a giant stepping across the planets.

In due course he spotted a wooden bench that fronted a picnic table. He strolled over and sat down. The park seemed deserted of human life. He heard the rattling and buzzing sounds of crickets and cicadas, and the weird sounds that squirrels made. He thought he saw a rabbit in the distance. He heard an owl.

He didn't know how long he sat there leaning against the wooden table, but his eyelids started to burn. His body felt heavy and very tired. He stretched out carefully across the bench, so as not to further incite the pain demons. Who needed a motel room? Within minutes he surrendered to the sandman.

CHAPTER 9

The chirping of birds and the barking of dogs interrupted a night of black, sound sleep. Johnson sat up, rubbing his eyes with his hands. His head jerked around to check his surroundings, hoping to find himself on that sofa in Buffalo. But any hope that this experience had all been a bad dream faded with his rapid eye movement. He was in the same place as when he had fallen asleep.

In the morning sunlight, he observed a few women pushing baby strollers. *I hope they didn't see me*, he thought. *I must have looked like some wino passed out here.*

Elbows on his thighs, he gazed down at his sneakers, black and gray with the letter "G" stitched on each side, whatever that meant. *What am I going to do*, he wondered. *Where should I go?* At this moment, life felt as hopeless as it ever had. He reflected on the darkest moments of the past. The endless bickering of his parents, their alcohol and drug abuse, his father's death in a car accident, drunk and speeding, his mother's cocaine overdose, all paled in comparison to this current living nightmare. This feeling of being lost at sea with no harbor in sight overwhelmed even his worst life experiences, such as being released by the Braves due to chronic elbow problems, subsequently trying and failing with one after another minor league team in an effort to battle his way back to the big leagues, and hearing the doctor say that he had developed arthritis in his right elbow and that he probably would never be able to pitch again. Incredibly, none of those events, even the last one, compared with the deep, dark depression into which he was now sinking.

"Hello."

He turned to see a child sitting at the other end of the bench.

"Oh. Hello, little girl." He resumed his position with elbows on thighs and eyes downcast onto his feet. He had no time for some kid right now, he needed to think.

"I'm not a little girl any more. I'm five. On my next birthday, I'll be six."

He smiled wanly. "Sorry."

"Do you want to play? The swings are my favorite. And the teeter-totter." Her hands grasped the front of the bench as she kicked her legs back and forth.

He looked at her again. At first he thought she had asked him to pray. She slurred her Ls and Rs in such a way as to cause them to sound more like Ws. "Birthday" had sounded more like "buffday."

She had long straight blonde hair with bangs covering her forehead, light brown button eyes, and a wide mouth and small chin that gave the impression of shy warmth. She seemed vaguely familiar, but he thought it ridiculous to think that he had seen her before.

"No, I really don't feel like playing right now. I'm sorry." Where the hell were her parents? He could think of nothing less appealing at this particular time than play on a teeter-totter. As sad as he was feeling, he almost laughed at the very thought.

"I need to find Rags. He's my dog. Mommy gets mad when I can't find him."

"I thought I heard a dog barking a few minutes ago."

"He plays with Taffy sometimes."

Johnson tried to recall the direction from which he had earlier heard the barking. He thought it might have come from behind him in the trees.

"I think—" he began, turning his head to the left. But the child was gone.

"Fine," he muttered to himself. He stretched out on the bench. Parents shouldn't allow their kids to wander away. What if he had been a pervert? He closed his eyes. *I wonder if I have kids? I sure hope to God I'd never neglect one like that little girl's parents.*

The sun was beginning to feel warm on his eyelids even now at mid-morning. He tried to focus on pleasant sounds, like crickets and birds. Katy said that was a good way to relax and feel better.

"Hey, mister. Got any spare change?"

That certainly wasn't a pleasant sound. The gravelly voice emanated from a ragged, stooped man. A wino? What was a panhandler doing in this part of the metro area? They generally wandered around downtown Atlanta near the shelters and soup kitchens.

"No," said Johnson. "Get lost."

"I fell asleep on the bus. They kicked me off. I been walkin' all night. I just need bus fare back downtown."

He was turning a shapeless black fedora around and around with his fingers. He wore an oversized tattered black coat whose pockets were ripped, baggy black pants, an incompatible red-and-green flannel plaid shirt, and a black tie whose knot had come loose and which was stained with substances that Johnson didn't want to know about. Atop his head was sparse gray hair curling wildly in every direction. On his chin grew a longer gray goatee. His cheeks were sunken and his skin was wrapped tightly onto his face with reddish blotches. The impression of his face as a whole resembled that of a goat. He stank as though he had defecated in his pants.

"I can't help you," said Johnson.

"Just bus fare. An' I promise I'll leave you alone."

Johnson sat up, sighed in frustration, opened his wallet and withdrew a bill. It was a ten, but at this point he didn't care. He just wanted to get rid of this maggot.

The old man's eyes widened in amazement. "Why, thank you, sir," he said as he made an exaggerated bow. He started to walk away, then turned back to face Johnson. "Tell you what," he said. "If you come with me, I'll treat you to the best bottle of Scotch you've ever had."

"I hope you're kidding," replied Johnson.

"I could use a ride to the bus stop. My feets is weary."

Such an outrageous request should have drawn a hasty dismissal. Why Johnson even considered it, he could not imagine. He intently surveyed the scrawny hobo. *Are you serious?* he asked himself. *Have you finally taken leave of your senses?* That was one of McBroom's favorite adages, only he had shortened it: *Have you taken leave? Am I trying to prove to myself that I've gone insane?*

But how did this geezer know that he liked Scotch?

McBroom always had compassion for street people. They would wander into his bar, and he'd give them freebies. "How bad can they be," he'd ask, "if they like to drink?"

Still Johnson fought within himself for sanity. "You can't be serious," he told the old man. But those deep, dark eyes that looked as though they might have been gouged out emitted something strange.

"I'd fancy some Scotch myself," said the raggedy fellow. He produced a small, almost empty bottle of cheap peach wine from an inside coat pocket. "This rotgut'll make a good man's head explode."

Johnson continued to stare at him, now in a fascination he could not explain.

"Prob'ly why I fell asleep on the bus, drinkin' that devil's brew. I never done that before, fallin' asleep like that on the bus. I tried to explain to the driver, but he said since it was the end of the line and I didn't have return fare, I had to go."

"You're crazy, old man. How do I know you won't pull a knife or a gun on me?"

He spread his arms. "You can search me."

Johnson shook his head. "The very thought of touching you could cause me to lose sleep at night. I don't even want you to breathe on me."

"Tell you what. I'll give you back your ten. Just get me on the bus, that's all I ask." He proffered the bill.

This was unusual behavior for a panhandler. Could this guy be honest? His story made sense in a weird sort of way. What harm could it do to drive the old codger to a bus stop?

But this is beyond lunacy, he thought. *Why would I ever want to have anything to do with a wretch like this?*

The man stood there, continuing to penetrate his soul with those eyes. There was no doubt something intriguing about him.

Johnson gazed around the park. Kids were throwing Frisbees. Moms and nannies pushed babies along and gossiped. A dog barked somewhere. The trees were plentiful, lush, and pretty. This could be a good place to hang out until he came up with a plan.

Plan? Like where to eat? Where to sleep? Where to go to the bathroom? When to go to wherever his home was now? Finding Katy or Manny or anyone else he knew? It occurred to him that he himself had slept in his clothes and might not smell much better than this loser. He felt the sandpaper on his face. He was certain that his hair was a wiry mess. How long before the good citizens in this park called the police on him? Then he'd be rousted out of the park just as the vagrant had been rousted off the bus. And what could he tell a cop? That he had just recently arrived from the year 1981?

Finally, sanity won out. "No," he said. "Go away."

He lay back down on the bench, faced toward its attached table, and dozed lightly for a few minutes. When he craned his head around later, the grungy varmint was no longer around.

He sat up to clear his head. I can't stay here, he thought. He pulled out his wallet again, scrounged through, and found three credit cards. Nothing fancy, just the standard Visa, MasterCard, and American Express. What do you know, he mused, something hasn't changed since 1981.

He decided to drive to a motel and see if those credit cards worked. If so, he'd get a room and take a shower, plus spend some money to buy new clothes. He walked toward the park entrance where he had left his station wagon.

Incredibly, the old codger in tattered garments was standing beside the passenger door, glaring at him while turning that old black hat round and round. Johnson halted in his tracks. He shuddered. How could this creep have known where he was parked? Or what he was driving? Had he been watching him yesterday and the night before? This was beyond weird.

"Okay, you old fart!" Johnson said as he approached him, his fists unintentionally clenching and unclenching. "How did you know this was my car?"

"Lucky guess." His voice had the raspiness of a two-pack-a-day smoker.

"I told you to leave me alone!"

"I went to the Port-a-potty and got rid of my underpants. So's I don't stink so much."

Indeed, the smell now resembled common BO instead of feces, although no less sour to the nose. "I don't care! Get outta here, or I'm calling the cops! You're freaking me out!" Of course, he didn't know how he would make such a call since he didn't have a clue where the nearest phone might be.

Johnson walked around to the driver's side door, prepared to run the old coot down if necessary. But suddenly the old man's right arm was resting on the roof of the Volvo, and his left hand held a black 9mm Baretta. "I'm so sorry, kind sir. But my old feets just won't get me back to the bus stop. I must insist on your charity."

I'll be damned, thought Johnson. *He does have a gun.* He held up his hands, palms outward. "Okay. Okay, you crazy old bum. Don't do anything rash. I'll get you to a bus stop."

They got in, the tramp holding the pistol pointed at Johnson's throbbing ribs. Johnson thought surely the hand would start shaking, and then he could disarm and get rid of the bum. After all, this was only some puny wino.

They rode together in silence, Johnson glancing over occasionally to see how steady-handed the geezer was. He reversed his course on Lawrenceville Highway, realizing that in 1981 the buses stopped at the DeKalb County line, which meant a drive of about ten miles westward. He wondered, *Had this old coot actually walked ten miles? Even if he could have, why would he have done that?* The barrel of the gun held steady against his side.

Finally he spotted a white cement post that marked a bus stop and pulled over. He turned to his passenger. The gun was not there.

"Thank you, Johnson," he rasped. "Your kindness is—"
"How did you know my name?"
"Ah. Forgive me. I looked in your glove compartment."

Johnson puzzled over this. *When could he have checked the glove compartment? Maybe while he stood at the car waiting? Yeah... maybe.* But he could have sworn he had locked the car. Still, the old codger may have broken in somehow.

But where was the gun?

And... there was nothing in the glove compartment with Johnson's name on it.

The old man got out and paused at the window, noticing Johnson's confused expression. "You must excuse me, kind sir. I have you at a disadvantage." He poked a bony hand, streaked with what Johnson hoped was dirt, through the passenger window. "The name is Gooch."

Johnson gaped at the hand in amazement that this Gooch would expect him to touch it.

"Ah, yes, *ahem*," Gooch rasped. "Well, thank you again. I'll be on my way now." After a few steps, he turned back to face the frozen Johnson. "Perhaps we'll meet again." He tipped his shapeless hat.

He remained parked while he watched an Atlanta bus pick up Gooch and haul him away. Johnson's hands were shaking again. He needed a minute to think. It was bad enough to be lost in the future. But this Gooch character, he dared not take him lightly. Was Gooch stalking him? If so, why? The year 2008 presented too many questions and not enough answers.

As he drove away, he saw a scrap of paper that must have fallen out of one of Gooch's half-ripped pockets. He looked at it, and became puzzled at what was scrawled on it: "Redrock Elementary." *I hope that doesn't mean that he works at an elementary school, not even as a janitor.*

Perhaps it was time to forget the motel idea and find this Champion Duluth address and learn what kind of life Wilbur Leroy Johnson was living now. What if he had a family there? What if Katy was there? Regardless of Katy, anyone who lived with him could help him find answers to his predicament. Even if he lived alone, what better place to search for possible reasons why all this was happening to him than his own home?

He reached into the backseat and retrieved the street directory that he had purchased earlier. While there he had also bought a carton of Marlboros, although, curiously, he didn't crave a cigarette. Surely he would soon enough.

He had two observations about the cigarettes. First, the price of a carton was absurd. Thirty-four dollars! *Inflation?* he wondered. *I guess if gas is four bucks a gallon,* which he had noticed, *I shouldn't be surprised.* But second, they had kept the cigarettes under lock and key in a glass cabinet behind the counter. They even asked for his ID. *How old do you have to be to smoke these days? Fifty?* Any minute he had expected the cashier to bring out an inkpad and fingerprint him. Call the FBI to run the prints.

Thumbing through the pages of the street guide, he found counties that had been only farmland before his journey through the decades. Lines denoting streets zigzagged through these counties like spiderwebs. Round and round, often circling back into each other. A fellow on TV named Leroy—that's why he remembered the name—had once observed, "The reason Atlanta is growing so fast is that once people get here, they can't find their way out!"

He searched for Champion Circle, Duluth, in the index, and found it, turned to page 3313 , and placed his index finger on the spot. It appeared to be in an apartment or condo complex off Satellite Boulevard. Had he ever heard of Satellite Boulevard? He couldn't remember.

Following the lines on page 3313, he drove back up I-85 North. Exiting the freeway, he ended up on Pleasant Hill Road, where cars were packed as close together as riders on a New York subway. *Jeez,* he thought, *this much traffic at late morning? How many billion people live in Atlanta now? Who are these people, and why aren't they at work where they belong?*

Then he saw them. At first he thought he was hallucinating. Smack in the middle turning lane on this freakishly busy street was a squat Latina woman, holding the hand of a small boy while pushing a baby in a stroller. Were these people lunatics? Did they think they were in some little dirt village in Guatemala? The worst thing they'd encounter down there while crossing a street was a mule or a chicken! He drove on, not wanting to know what eventually happened to that lame-brained woman and her kids.

Where Champion Circle was supposed to be, he saw a sign that said Tall Tree Apartments. Turning in, he discovered a Hickory Street, a Palm Tree Court, then finally a Champion Circle. As the road dipped and curved like a carnival ride, he tried to note the building numbers. Finally he spotted a building on his left with numbers just large enough to be almost impossible to read that said "1762–1770."

Johnson parked in front of the building. He entered the downstairs breezeway and searched his keychain until he found the key that would unlock the brown downstairs door with gold numbers 1768 tacked near the top.

It was his apartment, all right. He had never been accused of being a neat freak. Katy had always cleaned up after him. The mess he observed presented a clue that Katy didn't live here. Silverware, a plate, and a coffee cup had not been put away. From the smell, he had had pizza, but he must have stashed the box in the trashcan in the kitchen, a rare moment of fastidiousness. The plate contained crumbs and part of a sweet roll. The cup still contained about half an inch of coffee, thick enough now to paint an antique armoire with. A knife and fork looked as grimy as if they had been used to change the oil in his station wagon. Yes, this was Johnson's place all right. He was surprised that an army of ants had not yet invaded the coffee table.

His eyes surveyed the cream-colored walls. A Playboy calendar adorned one wall, another clue that no woman lived here. He felt sad. What had happened to Katy? Why did it appear that he was living alone?

A couple of cheap still-life paintings, like the ones you could get at discount stores for ten dollars, hung above the sofa. On the wall next to the picture window hung a larger picture, some fifty inches by thirty inches, which was entirely black. He noticed a shelf underneath it that held electronic equipment, which he studied briefly without success at identification. The closest he could come to an educated guess was some elaborate-type receivers.

A remote control was lying on the seat of a gray recliner, but he couldn't figure out how to operate it. Its buttons showed symbols instead of words. No button said "Power."

He punched one button after another until one evoked some whirring sounds from the receivers, then a snap, and suddenly the black picture transmogrified into a humongous television screen. He had never seen such a clear image. It looked as though he could step right into the newsroom shown on the screen.

He still didn't care for a cigarette. He wondered why. Mother Nature, however, was calling. When he entered the bathroom, he encountered the last and most decisive clue that no woman called this place home: The toilet seat was up.

From the living room he heard two phones ringing. He quickly spotted one of them, which looked like a miniature walkie-talkie, on his coffee table. He opened it and stared at it dumbly. As with the remote, he fumbled with it. The top half opened, revealing a caller ID that indicated that the caller was one Jesse Shandley. On the bottom he noticed an array of buttons, some of which resembled a regular phone. But Johnson had no idea how to answer this thing.

He put it down and searched for the other phone. Moving a dark green sofa pillow off an end table revealed a telephone he could handle. It had a normal handset and normal push buttons. A little white box next to this phone, another caller ID mechanism, was thankfully consistent in showing Jesse Shandley to be the caller.

Johnson answered it. "Hello?"

"Bad News, my man! I almost give up on you and hung up!"

Who started a conversation by saying that he had bad news to report? And what's more, this guy sounded cheerful, as though he was certain that Johnson could hardly wait to hear this bad news.

"Um, sorry, I was in the—ah—bathroom."

"All right. Takin' care of business."

"What… uh… uh… " Johnson was nonplussed. Shouldn't he ask what the bad news was?

"Just callin' to see if you're okay. Haven't seen you for a few days. I just thought I'd check on you. Make sure you haven't sworn off or anything radical like that, you know."

"I don't know, um, Jesse. I'm a little under the weather."

"Oh. Okay. Well, if you get to feelin' better, I reckon I'll see you."

"What was the bad news you were talking about?"

There was a pause. "I ain't got any bad news, man," he said, "I'm just *talkin'* to Bad News. I'm sure if you're *lookin'* for bad news, ain't nobody better than you to find it! Just make sure none of it blows my way! *Hah-hah!*"

Johnson forced a chuckle. "Yeah, *heh-heh*. Yeah, I'll do that. Look, I gotta go."

"No problem. Feel better, man. By the way, that hunk of junk still runnin' okay?"

"Yeah, yeah, it—it's fine."

"It's amazin.' I never woulda give it another week before it collapsed into a pile o' nuts and bolts. If you ain't the damn luckiest—well, anyways, I'm glad you ain't on your deathbed."

"Yeah. Right."

After he hung up, he stood in the living room shaking from the top of his head to the tips of his toes. He struggled for breath. Anxiety had attacked again, was going to take down blood and bones and leave him a shuddering heap of flesh on the floor. He sat on the sofa and breathed hard, filling his lungs with air as though he needed to over-inflate a leaky tire, causing his ribs to hurt more. The words flowed through his mind like an old-fashioned ticker tape.

What did this Jesse mean, he was talking to "bad news"? *Nobody better than me could find bad news?* The words confused and unsettled him. It was as though in 2008 people spoke some variant of the English language that he wasn't familiar with.

He knew what he wanted now, what he needed now. He explored the kitchen. Still no craving for a cigarette, but he definitely wanted a stiff drink. It was time to stick a fork in these endless aches and pains. Ignoring the greasy pots and pans in the sink, he opened cabinet after cabinet until he found a bottle of Scotch.

Just the feel of alcohol warming first his esophagus and then his stomach delivered him to a place of ecstasy. He drained one shot and poured another. And then another. By the time he had halfway emptied the bottle, he had moved to the living room, chased the one remaining lumpy cushion off the sofa, stretched out with his head resting on one arm, and stared at that large strange TV. He saw a soccer game.

With this TV, I'd have seen it if I were half blind, he thought. Until the consumption of Scotch began to double his vision, he thought he could count every blade of grass. He passed out there.

His last thought was, *Where the hell is Katy?*

CHAPTER 10

The blaring phones wrested him awake from his drunken stupor, but not before the answering machine had clicked on. Disoriented, he heard the sound of his own voice: "Hi. This is Bad News Johnson. Do your thing."

"Bad News Johnson"? That's what people called him? That solved the mystery of Jesse Shandley's call.

"Mr. Johnson," said a clipped voice. "This is Malik. Please get in touch with me right away. My understanding was that you would be back at work today."

Hm, he thought. *I've got a job. Where?* He checked caller ID. The call had emanated from a place called Clyde's Closeouts. *Wonder what they sell in a place like that?*

I've gotta call him, Johnson concluded, but he wasn't enthusiastic about it. This Malik had some sort of accent, Indian probably. But beyond that, he sounded like a first-rate tight-ass. Plus, he himself felt hung over and nauseous, having slept only a couple of hours since his Scotch binge. *What the hell am I gonna say? Oh, well. Here goes.* He dialed the number shown on the caller ID. "Mr. Malik? Hi, this is Johnson."

"Mr. Johnson. We were expecting you at work today. Am I mistaken? Didn't you request three days?"

Ad-lib time, heavy duty. "Uh, yeah. It's just that I woke up sick this morning."

"And when did you intend to call in sick, Mr. Johnson?"

"Right after I stopped throwing up."

Johnson could hear shuffling papers. "I never asked you the nature of your family emergency. An employee calls after ten at night, I assume those details can wait. But I do need to make my reports. Could you explain the emergency to me?"

Having no idea what the nature of his emergency had been, he lied, "Uh, yeah, sure. My mother is seriously ill. She's got cancer. Lung cancer. Her condition got really bad a few days ago, and they called the family in. When they do that, you know, it usually means the jig is up. But she managed to pull through. I think she's gonna make it. Of course, the cancer—"

"Mr. Johnson, I'm very sorry about your mother. But I still don't understand why you couldn't call in this morning. You have put me in a difficult position here."

"I—I guess I overslept."

Malik's exhalation took so long that Johnson wondered if he had emptied his lungs. "Can you come in today at all?"

"Uh, sure. I can come in later probably."

"How about five o'clock?"

Johnson readily agreed. He had wriggled his way out of the noose. Now he would simply get the Yellow Pages and find out exactly where this "Clyde's" place was. The feeling of relief regressed to the feeling of a march to the guillotine when he discovered "Clyde's Closeouts" in the directory.

These stores, whatever they were, took up a whole column in the book. What was he supposed to do now? Call each one and ask if someone named Malik worked as a supervisor there? He was dead meat. *Congratulations, Johnson,* he thought. *Been in* 2008 *less than forty-eight hours, and you've already lost your job.* However he had acquired it, Bad News Johnson was living up to his name.

Tossing the Yellow Pages onto the floor and replacing the phone on the end table, he slid over toward the middle of the sofa. The springs squealed in pain, and his bottom almost touched the floor. So he replaced the cushions, and climbed over to the middle one. The prototypical lumpy sofa. *No wonder I had thrown these cushions onto the floor,* he thought. He placed his elbows on his knees and leaned over his clasped hands in front of the coffee table. He could see scuff marks from many a heel of many a shoe; what appeared to be a smudge of some dark substance, maybe chocolate; plus a few water stains from failure to utilize coasters.

He had to try to think things through. *If I just arrived here… and yet I've apparently been here as far as everybody else is concerned… could there be another me out there somewhere? I know,* he told himself, *it sounds ridiculous, but traveling twenty-seven years through time sounds ridiculous, too, yet here I am. If I'd gone back in time, I'd expect to find a younger version of me. I have to try to find the other Johnson.*

His brain became tired. He stretched out on the sofa and soon fell asleep again.

The phone rang again. Glancing at the caller ID, his spirits skyrocketed. It was Katy!

CHAPTER 11

He had slept until mid-morning. She asked if she could come over. His response was simple: yes. His nervousness wouldn't allow further elaboration.

He cleaned up as quickly as he could, considering that his hands still shook, his head hurt, his ribs and joints were sore, his stomach felt queasy, and his annoying dizziness persisted. In fact, his whole body felt strange, from the skeleton outward. His bones vibrated as though struck by a giant tuning fork. Could all this be anxiety about Katy?

When he opened the door, he was struck dumb. Overcoming the signs of age was an attractive outfit with an electric-blue blouse and a softer sky-blue skirt that extended to her knees. Her black hair was cut in a swirl that extended to her neck. Her narrow brown eyes possessed that familiar glow that could energize the sunrise. In sum, the passing years had done nothing to diminish her beauty.

"Lee?" she said.

Hoo, boy. He didn't know what to expect. She hardly ever called him Lee.

"Katy?" he asked tentatively, not yet willing to accept the reality that she was standing at his door. After all he had experienced the last couple of days, he figured she might go *poof* and disappear or turn into a troll or worse yet, turn into Gooch.

"May I come in?"

"Sure, sure, of course."

She strode in, pulled the curtains open, and sat down on the sofa. "You're supposed to be in the hospital."

What hospital? he wondered. "Well—looks like I, uh, got better."

"Mm. Well, look, the reason I came over is to apologize."

He sat on his recliner in such a way that he saw only her silhouette due to the angle of the sun. He didn't know how to respond to this offer of contrition. Apologize for what?

"For the letter," continued the shadow.

"The letter."

She forged on despite the slack-jawed blank expression on his face. "The letter I sent you a few days ago."

"Oh. That letter. Yeah." He had no idea what she was talking about, but he didn't want to admit it. Everything about her made him uncomfortable. He cleared his throat nervously. "Don't worry about that. It's cool."

"It's cool? What's wrong with you? Do you know what I'm talking about?"

"Um. A letter?"

"What did the letter say, Johnson?"

Shifting around in his seat, he felt like a first-grader who had been put on the spot by his teacher and was scrambling to come up with the correct answer.

"I—I guess I f-forgot."

"Johnson. You could not possibly have forgotten what I wrote in that letter. Not if you've ever cared about me—about us."

"M-maybe I didn't get the letter you're talking about."

She sat back against the comfy pillow back of the sofa, turned her head to the ceiling, and exhaled through puffed cheeks as though a sense of relief had settled over her. "You haven't received it. Of course! *Whew!* Why didn't you say so in the first place?"

"I guess I was confused. But I don't remember receiving a letter from you recently."

"Well, just make sure if it turns up, throw it away. Burn it. Don't read it."

"Okay. That's exactly what I'll do if it turns up." He was shaking again. This Katy didn't act like the Katy he knew at all. She was so serious. It was hard to talk to her, almost spooky. Especially since he saw only a silhouette. She might have been a specter rather than a real person.

"I put some things in that letter that I never should have. I should've done exactly what I'm doing now—come over here and speak to you face-to-face. It was cowardly to put that kind of stuff in a letter. I like to believe I'm a better person than that."

"So… um… what is it you were trying to tell me?"

She looked down at her interlaced fingers in her lap. "This isn't easy. After all that's happened… no! I'm not going to tell you now. The timing stinks. Just promise me that if you get a letter from me, you'll throw it away immediately. Please!"

"Yeah. Sure. I'll do that."

"Are you feeling okay?"

"Me? Yeah, fine."

"Have you been to a doctor since you got home?"

Oh boy, he thought. *Another essay question on a test I haven't studied for. And why do I keep making associations to school?* After suffering through another hesitation during which his mind frantically searched for words, he finally said, "I'm fine. I don't need to go to a doctor."

"But they said that you suffered a concussion. They said you shouldn't have even left the hospital. You should see a doctor just to make sure you're okay."

"Oh, yeah. You're right. I'll go first thing tomorrow." *I wish I could tell her what's happened to me and be done with it,* he thought. This conversation was impossible. But what can I say that won't make her think I'm a lunatic?

Her already narrow eyes narrowed further. "Make sure you do, okay? Promise me?"

"Promise."

"Johnson, you're shaking like a leaf. Are you taking your meds?"

"My meds."

"Your meds."

"Oh—I'm fine now. I don't need any meds anymore." He thought she was still referring to the hospital and whatever had put him there.

She stood up with arms akimbo, glaring at him. She marched into his bathroom, and returned with a prescription bottle of Clonazepam. She held it up.

"You're supposed to take four a day. There's only four left in this bottle. Have you refilled it?"

Clonazepam. Where had he seen this before? "Oh! Right! I think it might be in Manny's car."

"Have you taken any today?"

"No. I told you I'm fine—"

"Johnson, you can't just stop taking this stuff. It could cause a seizure. If you're going to stop, you have to reduce the dosage gradually. No wonder you're shaking so much. You look like Don Knotts in *The Ghost and Mr. Chicken!* Take two. Now!"

"Okay."

She went into the kitchen and returned with a glass of water, holding two yellow tablets in the palm of her other hand. He wanted to lick them out of her hand, but chose to behave appropriately and plucked them out instead. While he swallowed them down, she sat down on the arm of the recliner, placing a hand on his arm.

"When Manny told me about the accident, I just wanted to come over and check on you. You're a mess, Johnson."

"Thank you."

"After that horrible accident, I can't blame you for being out of it. Get some sleep and get to the doctor, okay?"

"Will do." He wondered what accident she was talking about. It must have been bad and recent. He considered the scar on his face and the pain in most of his body.

She got up. "Well, I'll be on my way. I'll call you later. What are you going to do about a car? Is Manny going to let you borrow his for a while longer?"

"Um—I need to talk to him about that." Right answer? Wrong answer? Good answer? Bad answer? It must have satisfied her because it didn't provoke a response.

But he didn't want her to leave yet. As she approached the door, he got up. "Katy. Wait. How about a drink? I've got lots of Scotch here—"

Ernk! Definitely wrong question.

"Johnson! Did you just offer me a drink?!" She stepped toward him with fiery eyes.

"Ahhhh, sure. Why not?"

"Why not? What's the matter with you?"

"W-what do you mean?"

"What do I mean? Besides the fact that I've been sober for more than twenty years?"

Never much of an actor, he feigned absentmindedness. "Of course! What was I thinking? Tea, right? Or—coffee?"

"You must have injured your head! You're not acting like yourself at all!"

Speak for yourself, he thought. "Is tea wrong? I mean, you don't want tea or coffee?"

"What I want is an explanation. Where is Johnson and what did you do with his body?"

Drat, he thought, as the steel trap closed over him. *You don't know how close you are to the truth, lady.* "Listen. I'm just groggy. I just got up, okay? That's all."

"Mm-hmm." That tiny sound communicated layers of skepticism. Where was the Katy he used to raise hell with?

Who worshipped the ground he walked on? What had happened to her?

She strode into the kitchen and hooked up the coffeemaker. "You and I are going to sit down and talk! With coffee, not Scotch!"

He made no reply. He pulled a chair up to the card table that he used as a kitchen table, sitting across from her. He wanted distance now. This Katy might as well have been someone he had met this morning for the first time.

Her suspicion was palpable as she continued to stare at him. "Okay," she said. "Let me ask you a few questions. I want to see what you remember."

He remained quiet. The hissing and gurgling of the coffeemaker tranquilized him.

No. It wasn't that. His shaking had stopped, and although the pain persisted, his eyes had begun to burn with a relaxation that could have led him back to bed.

The meds, he thought. *It must be the meds. Nobody had meds like this in 1981. And I have a prescription! My own little treasure trove! These things are as good as booze. So go ahead,* he thought. *Ask me anything you want. And I promise that if it happened before 1981, I can answer it.*

"Who is Ellen?" she asked.

"Ellen, Ellen, Ellen. Well, I'm afraid I don't know who that is."

"Mm-hmm. Who's Marla?"

"Aren't you going to tell me who Ellen is?"

"Later. Who's Marla?"

"Can you give me a multiple choice? Like, a) your friend; b) Manny's wife; c) all of the above?"

"None of the above," she replied. "Let's try this one. Who's Zoe?"

"No clue. Sorry."

Now her eyes widened with disbelief. "Are you serious? You don't know who Zoe is?"

He felt the quicksand rising to his mouth. "Can you give me a hint?"

"Yes, I'll give you a hint! She's our daughter!"

The shock wave hit him like the fallout from a nuclear blast. "Our daughter! We have a daughter?"

She poured each of them a cup of coffee, handed him a mug, then doctored her own with milk from the refrigerator. "Johnson. You need to go to a doctor. Now. Obviously you've suffered a more severe head injury from the crash than anyone thought. You have severe amnesia."

He didn't even hear her. "We have a daughter!"

"Yes. Her name is Zoe. She's nineteen years old."

"My God."

"Better close that mouth. Something might fly into it."

"What if somebody told you that you had a child that you've never heard about before?"

"I'm just…surprised, Johnson. Even if you've got amnesia…well, it seems to be kinda selective, you know? You remembered me, you remembered Manny. I don't understand how you can't remember your daughter."

"Does she live around here?" he finally asked. That broke the floodgate of questions he had about this child. "What's she like? Does she go to school? Or work?"

"Slow down, cowboy," she said. "Okay. She's in her first year at Duke University. She plans to major in child psychology."

"I want to visit her. Now."

"Later."

"Is she pretty?" he asked.

"What do you think? Look at her gene pool," she said with an amused smile.

"Do you have a picture?"

"Sure." She fetched a large white leather purse from the living room, withdrew a red billfold, and proffered a picture in its plastic folder.

Zoe was attractive by any objective judgment. She had black hair flowing almost to her waist. Her almond-shaped eyes evidenced her Vietnamese heritage. Her height and her lower facial features, especially the prominent chin, favored him, he thought. Her wide mouth favored Katy.

"Does she have a boyfriend?"

Katy's expression became grim, snapping the billfold shut and returning it to her purse. "Not now. She's had plenty. More than her share."

"What does that mean?" he asked, now the protective father.

She sighed. "Let's save that for later. Right now I'm trying to get a grip on what you recall and what you don't. Do you know where I work or what I do?"

"No."

"Do you know Manny's ex-wife?"

"Marla?"

"Wrong. Marla is his daughter. Carrie is his ex-wife. Third—fourth—I lose count."

He rubbed his forehead. The medications calmed him, even made him drowsy, but they didn't kill the pain. His headache had returned with guns blazing.

"You think I have amnesia?"

"I don't see any reasonable alternative. Do you?"

"I just thought I had somehow traveled in time, you know, from 1981 to now."

"You think you're a time traveler? Johnson, that's ridiculous!"

"Katy, I want to believe you. Really. What a relief if this is just amnesia! But if it's amnesia, how come I can remember things that happened before 1981? How can you explain that?"

She pondered this question. Then asked, "So what's the last thing you remember?"

"You and me were sitting on a sofa in Buffalo, watching a car race on TV. It was July 1981."

She drew in a breath that stopped in her throat as though she had inhaled a bluebird. "How much do you recall before July 1981?"

"Everything. I remember everything up to 1981. So you see, this can't be amnesia. I remember 1981 like it was five days ago. It *was* five days ago."

"This is so strange," she whispered.

Johnson sensed that his message was finally getting through to her. "I can tell you where we lived up to 1981, the places where we used to meet for drinks, like Denny McLain's place on Ponce de Leon, your favorite restaurant just off Buford Highway that I usually couldn't afford to take you to, but I surprised you on the first anniversary of the day we met by taking you there. You didn't think I'd know that, you even cried. I can tell you the restaurant where we met, Chungking Charlie's. I can tell you about our first New Years Eve, 1978, when I got us a room at the Hyatt Regency downtown. We were partying with our friends, Gina and Patty and McBroom, and we all got totally plastered, and it was so cold, temperatures in the teens, and you were just blown away that I'd spring for a room in a place like the Hyatt. By the way, you never knew that I exceeded my American Express limit that night. I promised the desk clerk two tickets to the Braves' opening game."

"Some of those things I can't remember myself," she said softly.

"I think that was the night I fell in love with you," he said.

"You fell in love with me while you were drunk."

Now he was pissed. "And you didn't? You didn't fall for me when you were drunk? And be careful before you answer that because to me it was just a couple of years ago, and as I recall, you were drunk most of the time!"

"You're exaggerating."

This is a no-win fight, he told himself. *She has so little memory of those days. Leave it be.* "Next question. No, wait. I have one. You told me who Marla is, but you haven't told me who this Ellen is."

"Was."

"What?"

"Who she was."

"Okay, so who was she?"

"A little girl," she replied in a small voice that could have been mistaken for that of a little girl herself. "Marla's daughter. Manny's granddaughter. Last Tuesday night she was killed in an automobile accident. Your car burst into flames. You managed to get out, but not Ellen or her cat or dog. You survived."

"My God!" he said breathlessly. *That must be the cause of all my physical pain.* "Was it—m-my fault?"

"No. Some stupid drunk was going west in the eastbound lanes of I-20 outside Augusta and slammed into you. It wasn't your fault at all."

"I wasn't… drinking?"

"Believe it or not, no, you weren't."

"My car caught fire? How was I able to get out of it?"

"That I don't know. I haven't yet heard all the details."

"You're saying that this child burned to death? My God! Surely I wouldn't have left that kid in the car to die! What kind of monster am I?" A self-loathing descended upon Johnson as though he were in the middle of an imploding building. "How old was she?" Words were having a tough time making it through his throat.

"She was five."

Johnson creased his brow. She was five. That statement rang a distant bell. He poured himself some more black coffee. He wanted to be alert now. "So you knew her pretty well?" He felt desperate for more information about this child and that horrible car wreck.

"Well, of course, I knew her through Manny. And also, I don't suppose you'd know this, I'm an elementary-school counselor at Redrock Elementary School. Ellen was in kindergarten there last year. She would've been in first grade starting next Monday. But to tell you the truth, I didn't actually know her all that well. She was never referred to me for any problems."

Johnson's mind was whirring like a small child's spinning top. He began to understand all of those associations his mind had been making with elementary school. And somewhere he had heard of Redrock, he was sure. So Katy had become a counselor. *Maybe that's why I'm feeling like I'm stretched out on a divan while Sigmund Freud's behind me taking notes*, he thought.

What an intelligent, well-educated Katy I've got here, he thought. She couldn't be more different from the way she had been. Never would he have foreseen her in this role. *How did she get here?* he wondered.

"So how have I rated as a parent?" he asked.

As she gazed out the window, she replied, "Let's not go there right now. Let's just say it was the subject of many a quarrel."

He considered this last. *Quarrels*, he thought. *We never fought. I can't recall a single time we got that mad at each other.*

Something else she had said… what was it? It had something to do with… age? Whose age? Ellen? Five. *That was it.* "She was five," *Katy had said. Five years old. Why did that sound familiar?* Then it occurred to him. A child on a park bench who had told him, "I'm five. On my next birthday, I'll be six."

"What did she look like?" he asked.

"Who?"

"This Ellen kid."

Katy had not finished her description before Johnson interrupted. "What would you say if I told you that I think I saw her in a park yesterday morning?"

Her eyes froze on him for a long time. Just as he was beginning to wonder if she had turned into a robot whose battery had run down, she spoke again, "I'd say this is all the more reason you need to go to a doctor. Johnson, none of this makes any sense! Listen, 1981 wasn't five days ago, it was twenty-seven years ago! I don't know what's happened to you, but you need a thorough examination by somebody who can find out!"

"But not a shrink!" he added. "I'm not crazy!"

"I want you to see Dr. Pfeiffer. Susan Pfeiffer? Do you remember her?"

"No. Is she a headshrinker?"

"Stop talking like a caveman. And no, she's not a psychiatrist. She's a neurologist and neuropharmacologist."

"A neuropharma…whatsit?"

"A neuropharmacologist. She's an expert on the effects of drugs on the nervous system. That's how I got to know her. I work with kids who take prescription drugs or whose doctors want to prescribe them."

"So what's that got to do with me?"

"If you've suffered a brain injury that's caused amnesia, I think Susan's probably the best place to start."

He continued to marvel at the way she talked. *In 1981,* he thought, *she was a high school dropout.* "Okay. If you think she's the right person. I need to know what's going on. If you think she can figure it out—that'll be a relief, man."

"I'll call her today and make an appointment. With any luck she'll see you tomorrow."

"Tomorrow? On a Saturday?"

"For me—for us—she'll do it if she can."

"For us? She knows me?"

"She knows about you. She knows you through me."

That comment brought Johnson back to the disturbing fact that they no longer lived together. He decided to mine for information that he had little doubt would open a dark and foreboding shaft. "So tell me," he said. "Did we get married?"

"Yes."

"Are we divorced? Separated? What?"

"We're divorced."

A huge stone fell on Johnson's heart. "When did we get married?" he asked weakly.

"We started dating in 1978 and got married in 1983. We separated in 2005. We divorced last year."

"Want to tell me why?"

"Not now, Johnson. It's a long story. Three decades long, you know."

"No… I don't know. That's my problem. I have 1981 feelings in a 2008 world."

Her eyes met his with softness for the first time since she had arrived at his apartment. "I wish I could help you with that, but I can't."

They sipped their coffee in silence. "Okay," said Johnson. "One last question."

"Shoot."

"Did I ever make it back to the big leagues?"

She turned her head to avoid his pleading eyes. "No," she said.

That single word fell on him like a crashing Boeing 707 and left its debris in the farthest reaches of his heart. He decided that he wouldn't ask any more questions. Bad News Johnson had heard enough bad news for one day.

But with that thought he recalled another question that needed answering. "Why do people call me 'Bad News Johnson'?"

"I don't know all the details. Seems you were at a bar and lost your temper and got into a fight with some big galoot twice your size. But you managed to beat the living daylights out of him."

"I what?"

"He must have been pretty unpopular. Everybody else at the bar swore it was self-defense, so you weren't prosecuted."

"One fight? That's all it took for everybody to lay that name on me?"

"My understanding is that he was a real brute. It was like a David and Goliath thing. And you almost killed him with your bare hands. Manny said your face changed into what looked like a skull from a horror movie. Your mouth was grinning, but your eyes were angry. He said you looked like Satan."

"That's incredible. Who witnessed this?" He was holding out hope that this was some stupid rumor.

"Manny, of course. That guy Iggy. Your other bar friends."

"Bar friends?"

"You spent almost every night with them."

And not with my wife and daughter, he thought. *Check off one reason we're divorced.*

"Johnson, most people don't consider you to be a very nice person these days."

"Present company included?"

"Present company included."

Long after Katy had left, Johnson continued to sit at the kitchen table, staring at nothing. In all the years he had known Katy Nguyen, that had been the most awful conversation he had ever had with her.

CHAPTER 12

As Katy drove from Johnson's apartment, her mind could not detach from his predicament. *If he had truly lost his memory for all events since* 1981, *who is he now?* she wondered. For twenty-five years she had lived with his dark side. She could barely remember the 1981 version of Johnson.

He had been sad rather than mean—sad because his arthritic elbow had shattered his only ambition in life, to pitch in the major leagues. After the Atlanta Braves had released him in 1980, she had followed him to Toledo, Winston-Salem, Buffalo, and San Antonio, where he had tried to pitch for minor league teams to keep his hopes alive. Finally, they both had had to admit that his quest was futile. Ironically, it was in Buffalo where she had first begun to suggest as much to him. They had ultimately returned to Atlanta and had gotten married in 1983. That had marked the beginning of their troubles. While she returned to school, he turned to the bottle.

But if he were telling the truth—that meant that he had regressed. He was twenty-one years old again.

She thought about the night they had met. Johnson was eighteen years old then. He had risen meteorically through the Braves' minor league system on the wings of a one-hundred-miles-per-hour fastball. Katy was seventeen, a year too young to be working at an establishment that sold alcohol. But she had obtained a phony ID through her friend Patty's Uncle Mort—"Mort the Snort," as his acquaintances referred to him because of his dealings in cocaine. The ID had enabled her to work at Chungking Charlie's as a waitress.

Katy had run away from home to get away from her alcoholic and abusive father. Her mother was dead. She didn't know how that had happened. Her father had called her mother a whore.

♦

The night was passing slowly at Charlie's. *Where is everybody?* she wondered. *Surely not at the Braves game.* Their record was 57–90. She caught herself peeking at the clock so often that she was beginning to believe that its battery was dying, so slowly were the hands moving.

Her tables empty, she lounged at the bar, resting both arms on her empty, round, stainless-steel tray. She liked the way the bar had been decorated, with its dim lighting provided by half a dozen lamps with red square shades and its South Seas ambience. The seashells that were suspended from fishnets that criss-crossed the low ceiling grabbed one's attention and tended not to let go, much the same effect as staring at a large body of water. Plaques along the walls held plastic fish of numerous different species. Model ships in a variety of sizes were placed around the room, and a mural of a tall ship sailing the high seas filled three walls. In the background, traditional Hawaiian music sounded like a calliope played with a soothing, swaying rhythm. Okay, all of this was Polynesian, not Chinese, and Chungking was in China, but no one seemed to care about that.

Three men entered the bar. All were tall, one black—she recognized him as a Braves player named Brock. One was red-haired and slightly more heavyset than the others. This one was Manny, an off-duty bartender. The other guy she didn't know. He had long, curly, dark-brown hair, dark-brown eyes, a broad, easy smile, and a good square chin. He caught Katy's eye. When he looked over at her, she realized she had been gaping at him. She turned away.

Two of the men ordered drafts from tonight's bartender, a wisecracking, slender, forty-ish Korean woman called Lucy, while the object of Katy's admiration ordered Scotch and water.

"So you don't think you're going to get a chance to play, Lee?" asked the black man. "Why not? They wouldn't have called you up if they didn't want to take a look at you."

"Maybe I'm just being pessimistic," replied this Lee.

"'Course you are," piped up Manny, whose carrot top hair and red handlebar moustache looked as though they would intimidate any comb or brush. "You're one o' their best prospects. Did you see that in Daly's *Sports Daily* this week? Seventh in the organization. That's where they ranked you."

"Manny," said the cute one, trying to be patient. "Being the seventh best prospect in an organization that's finished last three years in a row isn't gonna cause Cooperstown to start making room for my picture on their walls."

"What is Cooperstown?" interjected Lucy while she washed glasses behind the bar.

"It's the Hall of Fame," said Lee. "Where only the greatest players go."

Katy, without looking up, could hardly restrain her enthusiasm. *They're Braves players!* she thought. She knew that McBroom had forever nursed an ambition to play for the Braves, and befriended as many players as he could in hopes of getting a tryout with the team. She was pleasantly surprised that his current Braves acquaintances included this handsome one. Exclamation points danced in her head. She might be able to hook up with them later at George's party. *But wait,* the common sense side of her brain argued. *If they're Braves players, what are they doing here? There's a game going on.*

As she tried to tune in to their conversation, her concentration was broken by the arrival of another waitress at the bar. She was blonde and big-breasted, and her vapid expression made her face look like that of a blow-up doll, or, some might say, a bimbo. "Bartendress! Bartendress!" she called, ready to place an order.

Lucy mumbled to her three customers, "See what we gotta put up with?"

"That's Cammie," McBroom explained to his friends. "Not the brightest star in the sky."

Soon Katy caught enough of the players' talk to understand the situation. The man they called Lee Johnson was a September call-up, and he wasn't scheduled to report until the next day. Brock Cypress, their only all-star the previous season, had been on the disabled list since June, following a severe concussion resulting from a collision at home plate.

Manny McBroom made friends easily because he always was the joker in the deck. Amid the clinking glass, the hum of other customers, and "We're Going to a Huki-La" over the music system, Katy couldn't hear everything he was saying, but his remarks consistently drew laughter from his companions.

She had forgotten her tables. But her four remained empty. The bimbo had six fat middle-aged men, toothless country folk, in the big city for a NASCAR race. Katy heard Lucy say, "Add up all seven of those IQs and you might come up with a hundred."

She asked Brock and Lee, "You guys players? You play for the Braves?"

"Yep," said Brock.

"So why are you not at the ballpark tonight? There's a game!"

"I don't report till tomorrow," said Johnson.

"And I'm disabled," said Brock.

Lucy eyed him dubiously. Customers would tell her anything, and she had heard it all. "You look fine to me."

"He bumped his head," said Manny.

"Awww," groaned Lucy, smiling, sure now that they were putting her on. "I bump my head *every* day."

Johnson, who had finished his Scotch, leaned over to Manny. "You gonna have another one?"

"I dunno, man. I told the little woman I'd be home by—" He checked his wristwatch, then continued, crestfallen. "Five minutes ago. Guess I better split."

"You working tomorrow?" asked Lucy.

"Yep," said Manny. "I'll be here."

As he hastened out of the bar, Brock observed, "The 'little woman'? If I called my wife that, I'd have a brand-new lump on my head."

"You guys want another?" asked Lucy.

"What d'you say, Brock? One more for the road?"

Cypress slapped him on the shoulder. "'Fraid not, pal. My doctor doesn't want me drinking any of this stuff with those new pills he's got me on." He slid off the barstool. "See you tomorrow."

"Oh, I get it. You guys are making me the fish."

Cypress expelled a deep baritone laugh. "Hey, it's not my fault she put us all on one tab."

"You want *separate* tabs, I make *separate* tabs," sing-songed Lucy.

"He's major league now," said Brock. "He can afford it."

Lucy asked after Brock had departed, "What you mean, 'fish'?"

"The fish is the guy who gets stuck with the tab."

"*Ohhh*. So you wanna pay now, or you want another?"

He slid his glass to her. "Look what they've done, making me drink alone."

"Alone?" said Lucy as she tossed in another shot and filled his glass with water from a tap. "What you think I am, a 'lucination?"

He chuckled. "Sorry." He lit a Lucky Strike.

"You got me, you got Katy." She tilted her head toward Katy, who continued to hold the empty circular tray while leaning on the bar at the waitresses' station.

Johnson walked down to her end of the bar with his Scotch. "You look lonesome down here."

She waved toward the dining room. "No customers."

"You know what? I'm glad."

"Why are you glad? No customers, no money. I took this job to pay my rent, not to stand here all night listening to three cowboys."

"Cowboys? Not me. I'm as city slicker as you can get. As city slicker as a taxicab."

"What's your name, slick?"

"Johnson." He extended his hand, checking out her nametag. "Nice to meet you, Katy."

"Hi, Mr. Johnson. What's your first name?"

He shuffled his feet, his chin falling on his chest. "Oh… I dunno…"

"You don't know your first name?"

"I don't know if I want to tell you."

"Must be pretty bad."

"The worst. My first name is Wilbur—reminds me of a horse. My middle name's no better—Leroy—like Little Lord Fauntleroy. Just call me Johnson. That's what most people do."

She wanted to interject that Manny called him "Lee," but she didn't want him to know that she had been paying such close attention to their conversation.

"Fair enough. Johnson it is."

They moved on to the standard getting-to-know-you inquiries, such as, Where are you from? Where'd you go to school? Where're you living now? You like it there?

Their ritual meeting dance was interrupted when a young couple seated themselves at one of her tables. *Damn the luck,* she thought. Then a party of four college boys, fresh from the whoop and holler of a strip club around the corner, took another of her tables. Both she and Cammie were busy now. Ten forty-five, little more than an hour until the dining room closed, and every tourist in town had suddenly discovered Chungking Charlie's.

Johnson continued to lounge next to the waitresses' station. Lucy had diverted her attention to a bald, chubby man.

"Sorry," Katy said to him at 11:20, "we're getting slammed."

He started to get up. "Maybe I should be moving on."

"No!" she said too sharply, surprising herself as eyebrows rose around her. Then she said, "Stay put," more softly.

Johnson obeyed, but loaded up on Scotch as though he needed to store it in his belly for the winter. He was on his sixth drink and his fourth cigarette when Katy approached him, her tray filled only with an empty pitcher and half a dozen empty glasses. It was five past twelve.

Johnson made a buzzing sound. *"Ernk!* Your time is up."

Katy took a deep breath. "Got a spare?"

He withdrew a Lucky Strike and lit it on the tip of his own before placing it gently between her lips. After a long draw, she blew out a trail of smoke. "Just what the doctor ordered," she said. "We're not allowed to smoke when we're on duty. I was having a nicotine fit."

"So what're your plans for me?" he asked.

"You're not going to believe this."

"And you're gonna keep me in suspense until I fall off this barstool."

"You look pretty steady to me." And he did. Nothing in his face or body betrayed the volume of alcohol that he had consumed—no red eyes, no leaning against the bar to balance himself, no shaking hands, nothing. For a fleeting moment she thought of her father, Ray Wilder. He could drink endless quantities of beer without getting drunk. That was because Ray Wilder was an alcoholic. A chill went up her spine with any reminder of Ray Wilder.

She exhaled another stream of smoke. "One of my roomies is Gina Attmond."

"Gina—you mean she's related to George Attmond?"

"Twin sister."

"So you must know lots of the players."

"Not only that. It's their birthday. After the game, we're meeting at Four Aces for a party."

"I've heard about Four Aces. I hear it's, like, the party place of choice for the team when they're home. Who all will be there?"

"Me, my friend Patty, the Attmonds, of course, and whoever else shows up in a partying mood. That's usually a big crowd if they either win big or lose big… or win close or lose close." She laughed. "In other words, expect a lot of people."

"Sounds like you should have a great time."

She realized she hadn't made herself clear. "You're invited."

He drained his glass and crunched a piece of ice. "How could I be invited? I just got here. Those people don't know me."

"I know you. And I just invited you."

He smiled, extending his hand in faux formality. "It's a date."

♦

Four Aces on Luckie Street in downtown Atlanta was built in the 1920s, and was remodeled and refurbished by a string of subsequent owners. Johnson and Katy slid into a wooden, high-topped booth across from the bar. Katy lit a cigarette.

"So, Johnson," she said. "What do you do besides play baseball?"

He looked at her dumbly.

"Was that question too hard?" she asked, puffing away a long stream of white smoke from her cigarette.

"No, I just… you mean like hobbies?"

"Mm-hmm."

"Well, I guess… baseball is pretty much it for me."

"All baseball."

"Pretty much. You've gotta practice to be the best. That's what I want to be."

"I admire that."

"Well, I sorta fell into it. Whenever my parents started screaming at each other, which was just about every night, I went to the backyard. I had to do something, so I started practicing baseball. One thing led to another."

"You should send them a thank you card."

He chuckled. "Maybe, if they were around. My dad died in a car wreck. He was a lush. He was coming home from a bar when he apparently picked a fight with a tree. The tree won. My mom died about a year later of a cocaine overdose."

"I'm sorry."

"I'm not."

"No brothers or sisters?"

"My parents didn't love each other enough to make another one after me."

She marveled that he would talk about his family so openly with her. Or was it the alcohol talking?

"Tell me about your family," he said.

"Same as you. Both parents dead, only child." Actually she didn't know where her father was—probably living on the street.

"You're Asian."

"You noticed."

"Asia's a big place."

"I was born in Vietnam. My dad was an American GI during the war. He brought me back to the States with him. I don't know much about my mother, except my dad said she had died."

For a moment they smiled into each other's eyes.

"So, Katy, what else do you do besides make Chungking Charlie's a brighter place?"

"I practice being a waitress all day so that I can be the best."

"Touché."

She didn't know what that meant. "I just hang with my buds. Drink. Make merry. Did I mention drink?"

"A lady after my own tastes." He ordered them both another round. "So who are these buds?"

She tossed her left hand toward the bar. "Gina and Patty. They're the ones whose eyes are bulging like Wile E. Coyote when he spots the Roadrunner."

Katy leaned over, cupped her mouth with her left hand, and whispered, "I don't entertain much." Which was true since most of the athletes preferred the buxom beauties over the diminutive Asian girl. It was a heady experience for her that this man, perhaps the handsomest player on the team, seemed to be attracted to her.

♦

Katy attended every game for the remainder of the season. She and her friends sat behind home plate, from which vantage Katy watched Johnson through binoculars as he sat beyond the outfield. Pitchers stayed there until the manager called on them to pitch. The Braves' manager never called on Johnson.

After the season ended in October, they partied. They engaged in drinking contests, which she always won.

In February the Braves invited Johnson to spring training in Florida. Katy's alcohol intake increased, much to the consternation of her housemates Patty and Gina.

"It's just beer!" she remonstrated. "Who gets hooked on beer?" Hiding behind her bravado, however, was the reality of her typical breakfast: a beer and a doughnut, and her daily snacks, beer and pretzels. "You have to have beer with pretzels!" she argued. She also required five or six beers to fall asleep at night.

Late one night in the last week of March, during one of her typical alcohol-induced sleeps that was less like restful slumber and more like simple unconsciousness, the phone rang.

"This better be good," she slurred into the receiver. Her eyes were still mostly closed, and her voice was a husky whisper.

"I made the team, Katy! I made the team!"

Bubbles as from the head of a draft beer swirled around in her head. "Huh? Who's this?"

"Oh. It's me, Johnson. I hope you're not mad, but I just had to call somebody! I know it's late, but this is the best news of my life! I made the team!"

"I read the paper." That he was delivering this news flash at one-thirty in the morning accounted for her querulous tone. But could it be that he had actually chosen her as the recipient of the best news of his life? Dare she dream such? "You knew there was never any doubt, didn't you?" She lit a cigarette in an attempt at mood modification.

"Well, I thought I would, of course. I knew I should. I guess I just didn't want to get overconfident, you know." His words slurred as he spoke rapidly, excitedly. "Overconfident" sounded something like "orcomfunt."

Since lack of confidence was a characteristic that she had never noticed in him, she tried to picture him as overconfident. It was like trying to picture a whale swelling to three times its normal size. A whale on steroids. The whale that ate Atlanta.

She lay back on her stack of pillows and let the cigarette calm her jittery hands. *I wonder why they're so jittery?* she thought. She listened to him go on and on about what they had said about his incomparable fastball, what his salary would be, and all about his teammates, including the team's star player, Brock Cypress, who had been cleared by his neurologist to play again, and all of the myriad other assorted characters who would populate his new world, their quirks and their superstitions.

Johnson's emotional state surpassed elation like a Corvette would leave an RV in the dust. His voice expressed the excitement of a little leaguer on his very first club. Katy listened as he droned on. *Was this,* she asked herself, *what a girlfriend was supposed to do?* Did this mean that she was, or was destined to be, his girlfriend?

Then fate intervened cruelly in April. Following his first game, in which he pitched the Braves to victory, his right elbow fell victim to excruciating pain—pain that never went away and never allowed him to pitch in the major leagues again.

CHAPTER 13

Johnson paced the floor after Katy departed. Not even two more Clonazepam could calm him. Amnesia? His anxiety blended with excitement. He wanted answers, and answers awaited him around the corner.

He tried to watch TV. It didn't take him long to discover ESPN. He couldn't believe it. Twenty-four hours of games. Somebody was always playing somebody in some sport.

The commercials gave him problems. They were so short and fast. He usually couldn't figure out what they were advertising. What on earth did "dot-com" mean? His father had cursed all commercials. "Make them put up a sign showing the name of their product, what it's for, what it costs, and where you can buy it. Then off the air with 'em!"

He glared at the computer in his bedroom, which he had first mistaken for an extra television. But it had a keyboard like a typewriter. What a mystifying little machine. Since there was no remote control to turn it on, he ignored it.

He couldn't so much as go grocery shopping until he could find his checkbook, without which he not only didn't know how much money he had, he didn't even know the name of his bank. His fear was that the checkbook had gone up in smoke with the car.

Manny called at six-thirty that evening with tickets to the Braves game. Johnson figured a ball game would be a good, mindless activity, such that he could stop worrying about his appointment with Dr. Pfeiffer for a while. And so he went.

At one point Manny had gone away, then had returned with two hotdogs and two beers. Johnson accepted a beer and reached for a hotdog, but Manny pulled it back. "Oh, hey, buddy, did you want a dog, too? I can go getcha one."

Manny had always been a big eater, but now, with aging, supersized orders had produced supersized Manny. Johnson wanted to advise his friend to stop gorging himself, tell him he was risking heart disease and diabetes, but he figured it wasn't his place to meddle. *Besides,* he thought, *look at the junk food I eat. Who am I to talk?*

Johnson shook his head. "No, that's all right. I'm not hungry." Which was true—he still lacked an appetite. He seemed to want too much sleep and too little food, except at those times when he couldn't sleep at all and wanted to fill his stomach with peanut butter. More mysteries.

"You're awful quiet," said Manny.

"Mm-hmm."

Manny McBroom didn't do deep emotional conversations. The next words out of his mouth were curses he screamed at the homeplate umpire. "Guy's dumb as old Hornberger. You remember old Hornberger?"

"Hm?" Johnson chuckled. "How could I ever forget him?" Then that phrase—*how could I ever forget*—sent cold water through his veins. *Yes, indeed. How could I forget a lot of things?*

◆

After the game, the loan of Manny's Volvo ended. The big fellow needed to take it back. Johnson wasn't worried. If he needed a ride, he would have an excuse to call Katy or Zoe.

He walked into the apartment with the intention of collapsing on the sofa, when he discovered that he was not alone. Gooch was seated in the gray recliner, as unkempt as ever, shapeless fedora in his lap, his nervous fingers turning it round and round.

As before, Gooch smelled of a repulsive mixture of cheap wine, urine, and feces. He ran his free left hand though the sparse strands of gray hair as though he were slicking it down for a job interview. The sight could have been comical, but Johnson failed to find any humor in the sight of this old reprobate again.

"You!" said Johnson. "What the hell are you doing here? How did you get in here?"

Gooch held his bony, wrinkled palms outward in a defensive gesture. "Don't be mad, my boy. I waited outside as long as I could. Gets hot out there. Old man like me, that heat gets into my bones—"

Johnson grabbed Gooch by what remained of the lapels of his suit jacket and slammed him against the wall. "You didn't answer my question!"

"Easy, Johnson, easy. You live on the streets long enough, you acquire certain talents. Like picking locks."

In spite of the bum's repellant body odor, Johnson leaned into him so far that their noses almost touched. "You mangy low-life! I oughta call the police!"

"Please, Johnson. We need to chat a while. It's important. It's life-or-death."

Johnson gave him one last tooth-rattling shove into the wall, then let go of the lapels, afraid little bugs might start crawling on him if he held on too long.

Going through the motions of straightening the wrinkled black jacket and dusting himself off, futile efforts both, Gooch slid along the wall and back into the recliner. "Just provide me five minutes of your precious time. I promise you'll never regret it."

Johnson sat heavily on the sofa. "Listen, old man, you give me the creeps. How did you know where I live?"

Gooch pursed his lips, searching his brain for an adequate response.

"And don't say it was a lucky guess! There must be a thousand Johnsons in the phone book!"

"I know what others don't. I am, ah, so to speak, a prophet, Johnson."

"A prophet."

"Indeed."

"A prophet. Like in the Bible, you mean."

"That is correct, kind sir."

"A prophet like Jeremiah and Isaiah."

"Yes, sir."

To Johnson this man appeared to resemble a prophet as much as he resembled an astronaut. "I suppose prophet work doesn't pay much these days. You know, what with so few pharaohs around and all."

"Ah, you mock me, my friend. My outward appearance deceives you."

Johnson was certain now that he was dealing with a crazy person. And what made him all the more uncomfortable, this crazy person seemed to be stalking him. Was he supposed to know this Gooch character? Was Gooch playing him? If so, for what? If not, how did he know so much about him? "It's just that I'd expect a first-rate prophet to be able to afford a change of clothes at least once every couple of weeks or so. Maybe you're just not a very good prophet."

"As it says in the Good Book, in the Book of Revelations, 'Yea, verily, and he shall walk among you wearing sackcloth and ashes, and shall bring the Lord's wrath upon the Malachites and the Hittites and the Erudites—'"

"I want you out of my apartment! Or are you gonna pull a gun on me again? You prophets are supposed to be peaceable folk, right?"

"Five minutes, Johnson. That's all I ask. My warning is serious!"

Johnson glanced at his wristwatch. "Two minutes. And the clock is running!"

"You must avoid that woman! The one you call Kathy—Katy—"

"Katy?"

"She is not the woman you once knew."

"I know Katy's different. People change in twenty-seven years. But I certainly don't notice anything evil about her."

"That's because your mind is full of hope. The hope you have for that relationship, the love you feel for her, they cloud your sensibilities. She can cloak her true diabolic nature." He coughed hard, a honking sound emanating from deep in his lungs. "Pardon me. Too many of them poisonous cigarettes in my foolish days of youth."

Johnson stood up, rubbing his forehead, and walked slowly around the room. "I don't know what to do. I don't know who to believe. I don't know what I'm even doing here." He had to admit that the old man had scored a few points. Katy did act very different. And how *did* this reprobate know where he lived? Or where he had left his car that day in the park?

Or was it simply that Gooch was hypnotic? His deep-set black eyes had a way of capturing his field of vision as though they could fill the room with a dark net. Whichever it was, Johnson was beginning to experience pangs of doubt in his own faculties.

"I'm your best advisor, Johnson. I'm your only friend in this world."

Johnson stood like a statue, back turned to Gooch and those deep, dark eyes. Finally he said, "Get out."

"There's more I need to warn you of."

"Warn me later. You always seem to know where to find me. I need to think. I need to be by myself."

"She'll be invitin' you someplace soon. You must not accept that invitation."

"Go! If I need more of your kind of advice, I'll get a Ouija board."

"Nothing I've ever told you is as important as this, Johnson! You must not go where that woman wants you to go! You'll surely lose what's left of your mind! And more!"

Still not facing him, avoiding those strange eyes, he said, "What part of 'Get out' do you not understand? If I have to tell you to leave again, I'll pick up your scrawny ass and throw you out of here! Am I making myself clear?"

"Yes," said Gooch resignedly, rising slowly. "I'll be on my way. Just don't forget my warnin.' You'll be sorry if you do."

"I'll keep that in mind."

"She says you lost your memory. That's a lie. You are a time traveler. I know. I live in a world where such magical things happen."

"I still don't hear you leaving."

"You haven't seen the last of me, Johnson."

Johnson kept his back turned as he listened to the opening and closing of the door. Only when he was sure that he had heard the last of that gravelly voice did he open the door. He watched the stooped, dark figure stride across the parking lot, in and out of the shadows created by the lights, and disappear into the darkness of a grove.

He returned to the sofa, stretched out, and shut his eyes. *Gooch is my only friend in this world? That old fart? I might as well slit my wrists right now.* Within minutes he fell asleep.

CHAPTER 14

A thunderclap woke him up. The contrast between the lightning flash and the darkness in the room informed him that it was still nighttime. He sat up on the sofa, rubbing his eyes. *There ought to be a law,* he thought, *against thunderstorms in the middle of the night.*

The light in the kitchen was on. Had he turned it on? Left it on? He couldn't remember.

He staggered into the kitchen. Seated at the table, just tall enough for her elbows to rest on its top, was a girl. *The* girl. He recognized her from the park and from Katy's description. This was Ellen, the child who had died in the crash. Yes. She had died and she was here.

"Hello, Johnson."

"Ellen?"

She nodded.

Thunder boomed. He sat down across from her. "Am I dreaming?" It crossed his mind that that wasn't a question one would ask if one were truly dreaming. When you were dreaming, you never seemed to realize it.

She shook her head.

"Why are you here?" he asked.

"'Cause you tried to help me an' Rags an' Taffy."

He frowned. "I may have tried. I didn't succeed."

"We're all okay now."

He stared at her. How okay could they be if they were dead?

She smiled. "We get to play all the time."

"Sounds like fun."

"We have lots of fun."

His face darkened again. "I must have caused a lot of people a lot of hurt because I didn't save you. Can you go see your mom? Tell her you're okay?"

"I did. But I can only go in her dreams."

"So why do you come to me when I'm awake?" *If I'm awake*, he thought.

"'Cause now you need help."

"What do you mean?"

"Gooch isn't nice."

"Tell me about it."

"He don't tell the truth. Ms. Nguyen tells the truth."

"You want me to believe Katy and not Gooch."

She nodded.

"I want to believe Katy."

She stretched out her arms in the universal child signal that meant she wanted a hug. He went to her, and they embraced. Her skin felt so young and smooth. She felt so warm.

They pulled apart. "I have to go. I gotta find Rags an' Taffy."

"Will you come and see me again?"

She nodded.

Lightning flashed and thunder cracked again, this time knocking out the power. The kitchen became pitch black.

"Ellen?"

The lights came on. She was gone.

Or had she ever been there? He drifted into his bedroom, sprawled across his bed, and fell asleep immediately.

♦

The phone rang. He fumbled for the receiver, noting that the clock radio announced that it was eight o'clock.

"'Lo?"

"Johnson?"

"Katy?"

"You sleep okay?"

"The truth? No."

"Dr. Pfeiffer can see you at ten. Can you be ready then? I'll need to pick you up about nine thirty."

"*Um,* sure. See you then."

Now he was wide awake. He was going to get some answers. That's what he wanted—answers. He hoped.

CHAPTER 15

During the drive from Johnson's apartment to Dr. Pfeiffer's office, Johnson was quiet. His gaze focused on the tall new buildings of the ritzy Buckhead section in northeast Atlanta. Katy attempted small talk, but soon abandoned it. When they arrived, Katy accompanied him into the doctor's office. Even though as ex-wife she was no longer next of kin, and therefore not privy to confidential medical information, as a practical matter she was as close to next of kin as Johnson had. And Dr. Pfeiffer needed her help for this interview. And Johnson felt that he did also.

Dr. Pfeiffer was a short, slender woman, whose hair had turned prematurely gray. She wore it long and straight to her shoulders. She had light blue eyes that peered out from behind large owlish blue-rimmed glasses, and a wide mouth with perfect white teeth. She sat casually, her hands laced around her knee, rocking slightly in her chair. She wore the standard white lab coat, complete with name tag and pens in pocket. The usual examining table, complete with white linens, loomed over her shoulder. She had placed Johnson and Katy in plain straight-backed chairs side by side across from her.

Johnson pointed to the reception area. "I wasn't able to fill out most of those forms out there." His mood was guarded. How much did she know about him? More than he now knew about himself?

"No problem." She leaned toward him, resting her elbows on her knees. "I understand there's a memory problem."

"I guess so."

"Do you recall anything about the car accident? Anything at all?"

"No."

"How about your stay at the hospital? Katy tells me that you were in the hospital in Augusta. Do you remember anything about that? Any treatment or tests?"

"No."

She sat back in her chair. "All right. Why don't you tell me the last thing you do remember."

Johnson cleared his throat, readying himself to plunge into a narrative that would no doubt leave her startled to the degree of petrifaction. "Katy and I were in Buffalo. We were watching TV, and I must have dozed off." He decided to omit the part the beer had played in his drowsiness. "When I woke up—" He interrupted himself. He knew how the next part was going to sound.

"When you woke up?"

"I was in Atlanta. And I thought it was 1981. And then I found out it was 2008. It was Buffalo, and then it was Atlanta. Everything was different."

"What do you think happened? If you had to take a guess?"

"This is gonna sound kinda crazy."

She shrugged again and displayed a broad smile. "It's a crazy world."

"My first assumption was that I had somehow traveled through time."

"Your first assumption. So you don't believe that now?"

"Katy thinks that's stupid."

"Johnson," said Katy. "I didn't say that."

"And I didn't ask you what Katy thinks."

"No, no, I think she's right. It's just that there's this weird guy. He keeps following me around. He says Katy's lying."

"Tell me more about this guy."

I'm digging myself right to the straitjacket ward, he thought. He hadn't considered how wacky his recent life experiences would sound to a professional. "His name is Gooch. He looks and smells like a bum. But he knows stuff about me, about Katy, stuff he shouldn't be able to know."

"And what does he say about what happened to you?"

"He says I went forward in time. He says I can't trust Katy or any of my friends, that I can only trust him."

"Do you trust him?"

"I'd just as soon jump off a cliff."

"Katy, have you ever met this guy?"

"This is the first I've heard about him," said Katy, who had been staring at Johnson incredulously.

Dr. Pfeiffer turned back to Johnson. "How about your other friends? Have they seen him?"

"No. Are you saying he might not be real? That I'm seeing things?"

She shook her head. "I don't know. But you obviously don't like him. You don't trust him. You believe Katy, not him. I'm not sure it matters how he's come to know so much about you."

Johnson leaned forward, running his hand through his hair. He had left out something, like a scientist omitting a key element in his experiment. And this element might truly cause the good doctor to doubt his sanity. "There's something else… somebody else I've seen. And I know she can't be real—at least not in this life."

"That sounds intriguing. Who are we talking about?"

"A little girl who died in a car crash that I was involved in."

"I see. Do you know her name?"

"Um… Ellen? Is that right, Katy?"

Katy nodded.

"Where have you seen her?" asked the doctor.

"In a park the day after I woke up in 2008. And last night in my apartment."

At this revelation, Katy stared at him again.

"But you don't actually remember the wreck."

"No. Katy and Manny told me about it."

"Did she talk to you?"

Johnson related to the best of his recollection his brief conversations with Ellen.

"So you saw her last night. Do you think you may have been dreaming?"

"I've thought about it. I must have been. But it didn't feel like a dream. Not in the park either."

"So you believe she could have been real. Like a ghost."

Downcast, he shook his head. "I've never believed in ghosts."

She leaned back. "Quite a dilemma. You don't believe in ghosts, but it didn't seem to be a dream. And since we know she's dead, it has to be one or the other."

Her manner drew him closer to her. She was here not to be judgmental, but to offer genuine help. "I can't just choose which to believe. I want to know the truth. I want to know what's happened to me."

"Of course you do. So do I. So does Katy."

"So how do we do that?"

She sighed. "I think we need to start with what matters the most. For now it doesn't matter who or what Ellen is. Or Gooch. It matters how these people make you feel. And it sounds as though Gooch makes you uncomfortable and Ellen is reassuring. Like a bad angel and a good angel."

"You think they're angels?"

"I don't know what they are. I'm not a psychiatrist, but here's one idea. You've lost much of your memory at the conscious level. But those memories may be intact at the subconscious level. Gooch and Ellen may represent attempts by your subconscious to resolve the inner conflicts caused by the accident." She smiled. "Did I lose you?"

"No… well, yeah, maybe. But if I'm not dreaming, I'm seeing things and hearing things, aren't I? Like some kind of schizoid."

"You're being too hard on yourself. If we figure out the memory loss, I think these visions may go away."

His brow furrowed, Johnson nodded, but said nothing.

"Okay," said Susan. "Let me ask you this: Is there anything at all that you can recall between 1981 and the present?"

"No. Nothing."

"What was your life like in 1981? Would you say you were happy then?"

"I was happy with Katy. We partied all the time. She was the only thing that kept me sane."

"How so?"

He explained his vicissitudes regarding his baseball career. He described Katy's supportiveness as she followed him around the country while he tried to recapture the pitching ability that could return him to the major leagues.

"Was that why you were in Buffalo?"

"Yes."

"Did you succeed in making it back to the big leagues?"

"No."

"That must have hurt."

"That's putting it mildly."

"Baseball was the dream of your life."

"Yes."

"So the partying with Katy helped you get through that horrible disappointment."

"Yes."

Susan leaned forward again. "How do you think you would have felt if Katy stopped drinking? And went back to school? And asked you to give up your baseball ambitions?"

Johnson glowered. His face felt hot. He figured his very demeanor had answered her question. He was right. He was too angry even to formulate a reply.

Susan nodded. "You might have felt betrayed."

"Yeah."

Dr. Pfeiffer turned to Katy. "Katy, I brought you in because I want to talk about the period between 1981 and 2008. Such as, when did the two of you get married?"

"In 1983. In June."

"Where were you then?"

"We had come back to Atlanta."

"Had Mr. Johnson decided to abandon his baseball career by then?"

"Yes."

"I had?" asked Johnson.

"Well… I thought you had."

"But he hadn't really?" asked Susan.

"I don't think so," said Katy.

"When you joined AA and stopped drinking, what was his reaction?"

"I wanted him to join, too, but he wouldn't." She looked at him darkly. "He said he'd drink my portion."

"Okay. Now, when was Zoe born?"

"Zoe was born in 1989."

"How would you describe Mr. Johnson as a parent?"

"He wasn't helpful when she was a baby. He said he had a very sensitive nose, and he couldn't get near stinky diapers."

"And later on?"

"We had disagreements. He thought I was too strict. I thought he was too permissive."

"Do you two need me here for this?" asked Johnson. "Can I just wait out in the other room while you trash me?"

"I'm sorry, Mr. Johnson. But I truly believe that you need to hear these things. All of this happened. This was your life. I'm hoping that something you hear will spark an emotion strong enough to bring memories back to the surface."

He sank lower in the chair, stretching out and crossing his legs as his chin settled onto his chest. "Fine."

"Now, Katy, when did you divorce?"

Katy described the separation and divorce, Johnson's desire to reconcile, his promise to stop drinking, their dating, and her letter after she had uncovered his lies.

"Is that the letter you were asking me about?" asked Johnson.

"Yes."

Susan asked Johnson, "Do you recall reading that letter?"

"No."

"How do you think you would have felt if you had read it?"

"Mad. Sad."

"Devastated? Depressed?"

"Yeah. I suppose so."

Susan's eyes lit up. "And the accident. How do you think you would have felt after a tragedy that horrible?"

Johnson took a moment. His hopes were rising. Dr. Pfeiffer seemed to think she was onto something. "I guess… it would depend on why. You know, why did I come out without any serious harm but the kid was killed? How could that have happened?"

"So there's a chance you might have blamed yourself."

"I suppose there is. I don't know."

"That's a fair answer. I think I'd feel the same way. It would depend on how well I knew the child, what the exact circumstances of the accident were, things like that."

"Yeah. But they tell me I wasn't at fault."

"It must have been a relief to hear that."

"I just wish I knew for myself what happened."

"Right. It's easy for others to say that you should feel fine."

"And," Katy interjected, "you didn't come out of it without any harm. You had a concussion. You left the hospital before they could treat you for it."

"A concussion?" asked Susan. "Are you still having symptoms, like headaches for instance?"

"No. I mean, sometimes, I guess."

Susan leaned back again, and pressed her fingertips together. She aimed her eyes at the ceiling. Silence riddled with tension filled the room. Johnson wondered what she was thinking, but he didn't ask.

She asked Johnson, "Do you love Katy?"

"Yes! I love her like it was 1981! I'm not sure I even know this Katy I see now."

"She's very different."

"She's so serious! The Katy I fell in love with was a live wire, always the life of the party. Always happy." Or so he had assumed in those days.

"Johnson," Katy began. Her eyes looked sad.

"What?"

"I just don't know what to say." She looked away.

Now Johnson could almost see mechanical wheels turning behind Dr. Pfeiffer's brow. She curled up on the chair, placing her chin on her fist, the elbow resting on her knee. She looked impish and engaging. That so overused word *cute* occurred to Johnson. "I've got a theory. But I have to admit, it's way out there." She raised a finger. "Excuse me just a minute."

She left the room for an adjacent office. Johnson heard pages turning in a book. He looked at Katy, who shrugged.

When she returned, she sat for the first time with both feet on the floor and leaned forward slightly.

"I think your man Gooch is wrong. I don't think you're a time traveler."

"What do you think happened?"

"I can't be totally sure, but I believe you have a type of amnesia."

"You mean like partial amnesia? Is that possible? Because I remember very clearly everything except the last twenty-seven years. I mean, I know that's a pretty good chunk—"

"What I'm thinking about is called 'dissociative amnesia.' There are cases in which people, after a traumatic event or series of events, have lost memory of the recent past."

"Wait. Recent? But we're talking about twenty-seven years."

"I know. I know." Her hands made a gesture as though she were pushing away an unwelcome guest. "Your case, if I'm correct, is one for the books. Very unique. The longest loss of memory on record from dissociative amnesia is eleven years. You've lost almost three times that amount."

"So why do you think it's this—what did you call it?"

"Dissociative amnesia. Here's my thinking. The car wreck that killed that little girl certainly had to be traumatic for you, especially since you survived with what we may assume were minor injuries. It's like the survivors of a plane crash. They often have what's called *survivor's guilt*, which serves to exacerbate the trauma. But that's not your only recent traumatic episode. You also have the divorce. That's happened within the past year, and you wanted to get back together, but Katy very recently—about the time of the crash—said no. And then there's the letter. You may have read her letter."

Johnson shrunk back, his mind buzzing and spinning. "Okay, you've got a point. I have no way of knowing whether that happened. I haven't found any letter around my apartment, though. How would you explain that?"

"I don't know. But if Katy were so determined that you not read it, she must have thought that you'd be extremely upset if you did. Am I right, Katy?"

"You'd better believe it."

"Okay... okay," said Johnson. Talk about traumatic. This little visit was becoming more traumatic than skipping through time. He could feel his whole body shaking. "But the accident. Everybody says it wasn't my fault. And the divorce. What if that wasn't my fault either? It might've been Katy's fault. We all agree she changed after we got married."

"Yes, but I'm not talking about fault here. I'm talking about emotional reaction. And Katy did tell me that you had wanted to get back together, but she didn't. So think about it. You've got the divorce, her refusal to reunite, that terribly upsetting letter that you may have read, and then the accident, and the death of a child, and the fact that somehow you survived. All that could add up to one hell of an emotional train wreck. And that's not even mentioning the career problems you were having in 1981, and that apparently continued to disturb you deeply. I don't know many people, if any, who could cope with all that."

Johnson whistled. "That's some kind of—but are you sure?"

She shook her head. "No. I can't be sure right now. So much of this works, but I'll admit it's hanging there by a thread. But if I had to put my money on a theory of what's happened to you, I'd bet on amnesia. Dissociative amnesia, most likely."

Johnson was speechless. Had he been looking at time through the wrong end of the telescope? He didn't jump ahead, he had forgotten twenty-seven years behind him. "So you think emotional overload caused all this."

"You may also have suffered a head injury in the wreck. We need to get that checked. I want to put you in the hospital for a few days so that we can run some tests and observe you."

"A… hospital?"

"Yes. There are tests we can run on your brain. I know you're not familiar with modern medical technology, but they could be very helpful. Your case is just so unique."

"In other words," added Katy, "all the things they wanted to do in Augusta before you left."

"But if it is amnesia," said Johnson, "is this the life I've gotta look forward to from now on?"

"If it's dissociative amnesia, memory usually returns, often after only a few days."

Johnson felt his first surge of optimism since... well, 1981. It felt like an electrical surge, reanimating the deadness that had plagued him, the spirit killed by the frustration, futility, and hopelessness that he had been experiencing.

More than that, however, worry revisited him. If those memories were dreadful enough to have caused the amnesia, what would happen if they all came stampeding back?

"A few days!" he said barely above a whisper.

"In your case it might be longer since you've lost so much memory. But I'm just guessing. Like I said, to my knowledge there's never been a case exactly like yours."

"A few days," he repeated. The whirring in his head had become a raging hurricane. Whatever had happened to him had occurred less than a week before. His memory might come flooding back any day now.

♦

Johnson and Katy left Dr. Pfeiffer's office together. She would drive him a few miles south to Piedmont Hospital, where he would be admitted today.

"Is Zoe at home?" he asked. "Why hasn't she called me?"

When Katy didn't answer right away, he said, "Oh. She hates me."

"I'll talk to her," said Katy. "I'll ask her to come and see you."

"Tell her I'm Nice Guy Johnson now instead of Bad News Johnson."

Katy smiled. "You were never Nice Guy Johnson. That would be a stretch. But I'll talk to her. I'm sure she'll come." Katy thought, *She'll be intrigued enough by his condition—this dissociative amnesia—to visit him even if that's the only reason.*

◆

Susan Pfeiffer stood watching nothing in particular out her window, her arms folded, thinking, thinking, thinking. Had she been too rough on him? Had what Katy had told her about her relationship with Johnson, rather than her questions directly to Johnson, influenced too much of her thinking? She had been expecting a tough guy, but had she found a fragile fellow instead? A fellow too fragile for her confrontational manner about his past?

But how could she have avoided that approach? He needed to re-experience those powerful emotions. They were the most powerful tools available to pry open his subconscious and release the hidden memories. If the memories caused him suffering, professional counseling could treat that more easily than a dissociative state of mind.

But she was also thinking about Gooch now. Katy had never mentioned Gooch. Could this Gooch be a hallucination? Hallucinations could be consistent with a dissociative state.

She considered the symbolism. Here was a guy, Johnson, who had wanted to play major league baseball. That was all he had ever wanted. When that dream was snatched away from him almost as soon as it had been realized, he drifted, not for a few years but for nearly thirty years. Never holding down anything but a dead-end job, not even wanting more, reluctant to return to school, resistant to the notion of embarking on a different career, straining his marriage to a woman who had grown beyond her hard partying days.

Some might well say that Wilbur Leroy "Bad News" Johnson had become a bum. And that was precisely the characterization Johnson had made about Gooch's appearance, that he was a bum, only not just a bum, that there was more to him. Mightn't Johnson have made the same observation about himself? So was Gooch the mirror image of the person that Johnson would become? These thoughts had occurred to her during the session, but she had decided not to bring this subject up. If Gooch was a real person… who was he and what was his agenda? How did he know so much about Johnson's life? Yes, they would need to talk more about Gooch. But that would have to wait.

CHAPTER 16

Johnson's room at the hospital was a double, but he had no roommate at present. The previous occupant of the bed by the window had checked out that morning. Another patient would likely arrive Monday morning. Johnson was stuck here until at least then. They wouldn't run any of their tests until Monday.

He had hoped that Zoe would have visited by now, but she hadn't. His mind so boiled over with worry that he had to request a sleeping pill. *Just as well Zoe waits until tomorrow,* he thought.

Unless tomorrow turns out to be too late. By then the dam might break and release that flood of terrible memories. What if, when his memory came back, he'd turn back into the jerk that Katy and Zoe despised, just like Cinderella's carriage turning back into a pumpkin at midnight?

◆

He was driving down a two-lane highway in his Pinto station wagon. The sides of the road were thick with tall green trees as far as he could see. The road dipped and curved. He saw the silver sports car in his rear-view mirror, approaching rapidly.

Within seconds it was almost touching his rear bumper. He accelerated to sixty, then sixty-five, then seventy, but the Camaro continued to press him from close behind. Now he could see the driver in his rear-view mirror. It was a young, stocky man who had shaved his head. He was mouthing words that Johnson assumed were curse words.

Traffic in the oncoming lane was steady but not heavy. The hills and curves, however, made passing another vehicle a dangerous proposition. So the Camaro driver honked repeatedly, and leaned out the window, shouting, "Get that old bucket of bolts off the road!"

Johnson fumed. "What the hell does he expect me to do?"

Suddenly the Camaro darted into the opposite lane. The driver gunned the engine and passed the Pinto, narrowly avoiding an oncoming pickup truck as well as Johnson's front bumper. In fact, both Johnson and the truck driver had to slam on their brakes to keep from striking the Camaro, which sped ahead.

Johnson slammed the gas pedal to the floor. His car accelerated to ninety, still barely able to keep the Camaro in sight.

"Leave it alone, Lee," said Manny from the passenger seat. "He's just some punk."

The speed of the Pinto reached ninety-five. The chassis vibrated from the stress. "C'mon, Lee. This old bucket o' bolts cain't take this kind o' speed. Pretty soon the two of us'll be sittin' on the asphalt with pieces o' this hunk o' junk scattered all around us."

"I need a new car anyway."

After a few miles, Johnson spotted the Camaro parked in front of a bottle shop in a strip mall. He pulled in and parked next to it, then got out and waited, blocking the driver's side door of the other vehicle.

The Camaro driver had a passenger also, another young man who had accompanied him into the liquor store. They both came out with paper bags containing bottles. Both stopped and glared at Johnson.

"Outta the way, pops, if you know what's good for you!"

"You need to learn some manners," said Johnson.

"Shut up and move!"

"He's just an old man," said the other young man, who sported a blond buzz cut and light facial hair.

"If you apologize for almost running me off the road, I'll leave."

"Shut up, old man! Or I'll break you and that butt-ugly car of yours in two!"

"Look at that thing, Stan. Isn't that the stupidest-looking car you've ever seen?"

"It's what old geezers drive."

"You still have time to apologize—"

"Shut up!" Stan handed his bag to his friend.

Johnson walked toward him. "Don't say I didn't give you a chance."

"Lee!" shouted Manny. "C'mon, man! They ain't worth it!"

"Better get your fat friend to come out and help you. You're gonna—"

Johnson's left fist collided with Stan's nose with a blow that staggered the latter and drew blood. With his right lower leg, Johnson took advantage of Stan's temporary imbalance to trip him. Stan fell hard to the concrete. His friend ran.

♦

Johnson opened his eyes. He could see darkness outside the window. Ellen was sitting at the end of his bed, rubbing Taffy in her lap as the kitten purred loudly.

"Was that a dream?" he asked.

Ellen shook her head.

"It actually happened? I've remembered something?"

"Yes."

No wonder they called me Bad News Johnson, he thought. "What happened to that kid?"

"He can't see out of one eye. And he has fits."

"Fits?"

"He lays on the ground and shakes. And white stuff comes out of his mouth."

"Did they call the police on me?"

She shook her head. "They was scared."

He stared at the ceiling. The sleeping pill had worn off. He got up and walked to the window. When he turned around, the child was gone.

CHAPTER 17

Johnson came out of the bedroom, poured himself some black coffee, and headed for the living room. Katy, seated at the kitchen table, stopped him. "Sit down, Johnson. We need to talk."

"I'm not in the mood to talk."

"Neither am I. But we have to."

He sat down across from her. He rubbed his eyes, ran a hand through his disheveled hair, and wiped his mouth as though the skin on his face was too tight. He wore only a bathrobe and had not showered or shaved.

"Okay. I'm sorry about this, babe," he said.

Katy took a long slurp from her cup. "I want to know what's going on with you," she said.

He shrugged. "Just some bad luck. It happens in poker, it happens in life."

"You took our daughter out there and got her drunk!"

"She did that all by herself, babe. I don't know why kids her age can't drink anyway. It's less harmful than cigarettes, and all the kids smoke cigarettes."

"I talked to the police at the jail. If that cop hadn't been able to stop in time, he would have crashed into you. Zoe could have been killed!"

"But he did, and she wasn't."

She put the large white ceramic cup with its red script, "Children are for loving," which she had been holding with both hands, on the table and fixed an unblinking stare on him. Her eyes were so intimidating, like the steely eyes of a Marine in battle, that he turned his face away. "I want to know what all the drinking is about once and for all, Johnson. It keeps getting worse. You're drinking more and more and more. I think you're an alcoholic. I think you need help."

"I'm not an alcoholic."

"That's what all alcoholics say."

"Look, if we're gonna sit here and you're gonna accuse me of lying, then I'd say there's no point to this conversation."

"You know that you're drinking more now than ever before."

He took another gulp of coffee while his mind attempted to articulate a response that would cut her off at the knees. "Maybe," was the best he could do.

"Tell me why," she entreated him. "Why are you drinking so much now?"

He sighed. He failed to see the value of this discussion. *Okay,* he thought. *You don't want to hear it, but you asked for it.* "I hate my life, Katy."

"What specifically do you hate about your life?"

By now he had turned his whole body away from her in the chair. "I know what you're going to say if I answer that question."

"No, you don't. You can't know that."

Johnson's eyes narrowed as he thought, *We'll see about that.* "It's about baseball." Out of the corner of his right eye he watched for her response. Was she going to tell him for the umpteenth time to forget about baseball? Go back to school? Find another career? He felt as though he had heard this refrain as often as he had heard the sound of her voice.

But she deviated again from the script in his mind. "What specifically about baseball?" she asked.

"Katy, I've been trying to make you understand for twenty-five years. I doubt if I'd be able to do it today."

"Try me. Even if you believe I haven't understood in the past, what've you got to lose?"

He replied while he continued to look at the light blue wallpaper on the other side of the kitchen.

"I guess I've resented your ultimatums."

"Ultimatums? What do you mean?" Her voice contained a quiver. "I want to know exactly what ultimatums you're talking about."

Seconds seemed like an hour before he responded. He could hear the humming of the refrigerator and the ticking of the wall clock above their silence. "Okay, to be fair," he finally said, "I suppose there was just the one. But it was a big one."

"What was it?" she asked weakly.

"It was before we got married. I went to San Antonio to try and make their club. You said you were going back to Atlanta and going back to school. If I didn't catch on with that team, and if I still wanted to continue my comeback after that, you wouldn't stay with me. That was the ultimatum."

"Johnson! I—I don't think I ever said that!"

"You said it, all right. And whenever I've brought up baseball since then, you've gotten angry and told me to forget baseball. Now, at my age… it's too late."

She said slowly, "The way I remember it was that if you made it in San Antonio, I'd come and join you. But if you didn't make it, you'd return to Atlanta and stop pursuing baseball. That was our deal. There was no ultimatum."

"Maybe it was—what do you call it, implied. But it was there. I had to quit baseball to keep you. I had to choose one or the other."

"I've never put you in that position, and you know it. Why are you dredging up something that happened twenty-five years ago, anyway?"

"Because it feels like yesterday! It really hit me when I passed age forty. Then I knew I was too old. The dream was dead. Before then I couldn't choose because of your ultimatum. After age forty it was too late."

"You've never talked about this before. You've been carrying all this around for all these years and just now you've decided to talk about it?"

"I tried. Every time I'd bring up baseball, you'd get mad."

"Johnson, all I ever did was to try to help you to see that it was futile. Team after team dropped you. Your arm never came back."

"I could've made it if I had kept on trying! I know I could! But you gave up on me and gave me the ultimatum!"

"You made a choice."

"I had no choice! I loved you, and I loved baseball!"

"You think if it hadn't been for my so-called ultimatum, you could've had both me and a baseball career."

"Yes. That's how I see it."

"Johnson, I don't recall giving you anything like an ultimatum. If I made it sound like that, I'm sorry."

"It's too late to be sorry now."

"That part isn't my fault. You should have talked to me before, long ago, like this. You waited until it was too late for us to be able to resolve the problem."

"I told you, I tried. You wouldn't talk about baseball anymore."

"I don't buy that. I don't believe I ever closed you off like that."

"Believe whatever you want."

She sat quietly, looking at him as he looked away. "Okay. I guess we'll just have to agree to disagree about this. But I never intended anything but to be supportive."

No reply. He drank more coffee.

"Have you ever thought about coaching, like, Little League or something?"

"Sure I have. You've brought that up before. That's just not something I'd want to do."

"Would it hurt to try it and see if you like it?"

"I don't need to try it. I know I wouldn't like it."

"Johnson, working with children can be fulfilling beyond anything you've ever imagined. Take my word, it's at least worth a try."

He didn't reply. He sat stiffly, teeming inside, continuing to face away from her.

"In any event," she said. "We have another problem to resolve now. Your drinking."

"My drinking is not a problem."

"Your drinking almost got our daughter killed, Johnson."

Still looking away, wishing that he could take up smoking again, he said, "I made a bad decision there. I should've stayed away from the beer while I was with Zoe. That won't ever happen again. Problem resolved."

"I don't think so."

"Think what you want to think."

She leaned over, resting her elbows on the table, shouting with her eyes. "I deny that I gave you any kind of ultimatum twenty-five years ago. But I'm giving you one now."

That managed to turn his head.

"Either you get some help for your alcohol abuse and depression," she continued, "or I want you to leave."

He was dumbfounded, the shock of her words flowing into his mind on high-tension wires. He remembered once, while watching his father and mother argue, he had felt as though they both had electrical, highly charged wires sprouting from their heads like tentacles, connecting with each other and with him, filling the room and shooting high-voltage shocks. "You want us to split up?"

"Until you get some help, yes."

🜚

The room became darker, the light from the hallway blocked by a figure in the doorway. It wasn't a nurse. Far from it. It was Gooch.

"Remembering stuff, eh?" he rasped.

"Funny statement, coming from you. You insisted I was a time traveler."

"I lied. I wanted to keep you away from Katy. I knew this would happen."

"And what's wrong with that? What's wrong with my amnesia being cured?"

"Nothing, I suppose, if you don't mind becoming your old self again."

Johnson said nothing.

"You'll never be able to make amends. You won't have time. Your memory's coming back too fast. See you around, Johnson." He turned and walked away.

Johnson noticed Ellen standing in a dark corner of the room. "Is he right? I won't have time to win back Katy and Zoe?"

"No. Gooch is never right. I'll help. Me and Rags and Taffy'll help."

Help how? thought Johnson, feeling very tired. *By telling me whether Katy really did give me an ultimatum? Whether she ruined my career in baseball? Look who I'd be asking—a five-year-old girl! She wouldn't even know what "ultimatum" means!* He turned over in bed, and closed his eyes.

CHAPTER 18

It was Monday evening. Zoe sat at a small round table near the vending machines, sipping coffee from a paper cup. She was alone save the occasional young man or woman who entered dressed in hospital garb. She wanted it this way. She figured most patient visitors would be in the patient rooms or in the cafeteria.

Her hands shook from anxiety. She wanted to visit her father, but at the same time she feared doing so. Her mother assured her that he was different—not mean, not short-tempered. Katy had tried to explain the amnesia, and had described it more technically than she would have done for most teenagers. Zoe had entered Duke University, an institution renowned for its department of Psychology, on a full scholarship. Not only blessed with an IQ of one hundred fifty, she had buried herself in books from an early age to escape the tension in her home.

Why am I so scared? she wondered. *Isn't this why I chose to major in psychology? To understand my father?*

No. The purpose was to understand myself. And other children. Just as her mother before her, she had answered some inner outcry: Help them. Help the children. Help them.

♦

She got up and walked to the elevator. *It's not going to become less scary sitting here,* she decided.

When she entered her father's room, her first sensation was the loud, raucous sound of a television from behind the curtain of Johnson's roommate. The second sensation was her dad's prying eyes. *He doesn't know who I am,* she thought. *I might be some cute medical assistant.*

His eyes widened. "Zoe?"

She brushed her long black hair away from her face to rest halfway down her back. "Hi, dad."

"Come here, let me look at you."

She stepped tentatively toward him.

"You're even thinner than in the pictures Katy showed me. You don't have a health problem, do you?"

"No, dad, I'm not anorexic."

"You're not what?"

"I don't have an eating disorder. I've always been thin like this."

"Of course. Of course you have. It's just that I don't remember any of that, you know."

"I know. Mom told me."

"You could be a model, as tall as you are."

She sat on the visitor's chair at the front of the cushion. *Maybe for a quick getaway in case he starts yelling at me?* "I want to be a child psychologist."

Looking to his left, he said in a husky whisper, "I'm sorry about the noise. That guy watches wrestling constantly."

"That's okay."

"Do you think I should tell him it's all fake?"

"Don't do that. It's okay, really."

"Child psychologist, huh? That's great."

Zoe didn't respond. What could she say to such a generic observation?

"You can help a lot of kids someday."

"I hope so."

She noticed that he hadn't mentioned the rings in her eyebrows, nose, or lip. She decided to push her luck. "I've got a stud."

"A stud? Who?"

She couldn't suppress the giggle. "Not who. What." She opened her mouth to reveal the jewel in the middle of her tongue. "Got a couple of new tattoos, too."

"Yeah. Well, I guess that's what young people do these days, huh?"

She stared at his face for some sign of sarcasm but detected only wide-eyed innocence. "You tried to throw me out of the house when I got my first tattoo."

"I did?" His brow wrinkled.

"It worries you that you treated me like that."

He nodded. "I don't understand how I became that kind of person. It's not like I wasn't a pretty wild teenager myself."

"Mom says you were both pretty wild."

"Mom would be right about that."

"Mom told me about your amnesia, but it sounds really weird."

Okay, he thought, feeling like a cliff diver. *Here she goes.* He related as much as he could recall about that day that he had awoken on the shoulder of the interstate, totally disoriented, as though while he had slept a gang of engineers had hastily built a duplicate Atlanta around him, a place that both looked like Atlanta and didn't look like Atlanta at the same time because the engineers had done a sloppy job. And how he was supposed to be in Buffalo, anyway. He described his appointment with Dr. Pfeiffer.

"Do you, like, ever dream of things that might help you remember stuff?"

"I have some very bizarre dreams, but nothing that has helped bring back any memory," he lied. He rationalized the lie by focusing on the fact that the only people who had told him that his dreams were accurate depictions of the past were Ellen and Gooch.

She looked down at her interlocked fingers. "I should go. It looks stormy outside, and I hate to drive in storms. I love to watch them. All that energy is exciting. But I hate to drive in them. Besides the rain itself, the traffic always seems to be worse."

"I guess some things never change. Even in 1981, a few raindrops and people would go nuts out there. I swear there's more traffic when it rains. It's like people stand at their windows, pull the curtains back, and say, 'Wow! It's raining! Let me get my car and get out there!'"

"That's true."

"So it's raining now?"

"It was. Not so much now. But I heard a forecast on the radio that there's more to come." Talking about the weather—the last refuge for those with absolutely zero imagination. One talked about the weather with grocery store clerks or paper delivery boys or janitors. Even bartenders elicited more substantial conversation. Yet her own father's speech was halting as though he were reaching for words to fill up space. She felt as though she were talking to a stranger.

"So you're leaving already?"

"This is hard for me, Dad. Without all those years that you've forgotten, we don't know each other."

"I want to know all about you."

"Well, they say your memory will come back. Then—"

"No, not that way. I want us to spend time together. I want to know about your life now, not before."

"Okay," she said weakly.

"Promise."

She got up to leave. "Call me when you get out of this place."

"I will. When are you going back to Duke?"

"Not for another couple of weeks." She kissed his forehead. "'Bye, Dad."

"See you soon, Zoe. Take care."

As she walked toward the elevator, her shaking hand wiped away a tear.

◆

Katy visited briefly Monday night, but her emotions were wound too tightly after such a first day at school. She had no questions for Johnson other than a few platitudes. "How are you doing?"

"I'm fine. You?"

With rapid-fire delivery, she launched into a long narrative about the grief counselors, the teachers who had needed her help with crying kindergartners and/or crying parents, Ellen's friends who had needed to come to her office, and the first-grade class (not Tameka's) whose questions about death and dying needed answering.

Then away she flew.

Maybe she's talking to Dr. Pfeiffer, he thought. *Maybe there's something terrible they don't want me to know. Maybe she's nervous because she doesn't want to tell me.*

He scowled and drank some water. *A guy can get paranoid spending day after day in a hospital bed, listening to the World Wrestling Federation. Is there a TV station that shows nothing but wrestling all day 24/7?* At home he had found a similar station that showed nothing but golf.

Or maybe Katy was too self-involved to care. That was the thought that troubled him.

Maybe she could never love him again.

CHAPTER 19

On Wednesday Dr. Pfeiffer came bouncing in bright and early shortly after eight a.m. "Has Dr. Schroeder been in yet?"

"No. Who's he?"

"My associate. Well, never mind. I have some good news for you."

"Good news?"

"The tests don't show any hematoma, or any obvious damage to the occipital, parietal, or temporal lobes."

"English please?"

She chuckled. "No bleeding in the brain. That's a biggie. And they haven't found any damage to parts of the brain that would cause memory loss."

"So I won't have to stick my head into that stupid tube again?"

"I understand you had some problems with the MRI machine."

"You know, if they tell you not to swallow, you're almost sure to need to swallow."

"Hopefully we'll have better technology the next time you have amnesia."

"And what does all this say about my amnesia?"

"That it's purely traumatic. That means your memory should come back pretty soon, like we talked about in my office. The tests seem to have confirmed my diagnosis of dissociative amnesia."

"What about the hallucinations?"

"That's still the wild card. Pete—Dr. Schroeder—and I will have to put our heads together about the hallucinations. They don't exactly fit any theory. That's not so unusual. Like I said, there's so much about brain injuries that we just don't know. Have you had any more?"

"Yes. Saturday night."

"Who did you see?"

"Both of them."

"Well, don't worry about them. I still believe they'll go away as you recover more of your past."

He frowned. "If I tell you something, it's just between you and me, right?"

"Of course." She appeared puzzled.

"I've remembered a couple of things."

She sat down. "Oh?"

"It was very disturbing."

"Tell me about what you recall."

"Not now. It's just that… I had thought it would all come back at once. When it comes back piecemeal… it's confusing."

"I'm sure it is."

Perhaps her tone of voice sounded unconcerned. Or perhaps those two recovered memories generated more agitation than he could bear. Were all the memories that terrible? Had he been that terrible? Was there any hope that he could resist the impulse to return to the terrible person he had been? At this point he had nothing to hang onto. He was falling backwards through the air.

He shouted, "I don't know who I am! I don't know Katy or Zoe or anybody! I'm lost, doc! I'm lost!" He began to cry, covering his eyes with his hands. Laying aside 1981 to 2008, he hadn't cried since he was a young child.

Susan moved to sit on his bed. "I know you are. Listen, you're going through a lot. But there's no reason you should have to go through all this alone. You're going to need counseling. Katy can help find a good counselor. We're going to make sure you get all the help you need. And I want you to know that I'm here for you, too. When I go, I'm going to leave you my card. I want you to call me anytime, day or night, if you remember something else. We need to sort out these memories together, all of us, you, me, Katy, your counselor. You need to know you're not alone. They're going to discharge you tomorrow morning. I want you to go home, rest, try to clear your mind. Watch TV. Listen to music. Do what you like to do. If memories come back, disturbing or otherwise, call one of us immediately. Whatever my schedule is, I'll make room for you. Okay?"

"Okay."

She sat smiling into his eyes, and patted his hand.

"You see, my problem is this. The more I remember, the more likely it is that I'll turn back into the horse's ass that turned them against me. So I'm on a clock, and I don't know when the clock'll run out. I have to win them back before it's too late."

"You know what? I don't think you'll ever be that kind of person again."

After she left, he glared at the ceiling, his hands folded behind his head. He thought about the man in the other bed. *Did I embarrass myself? I'd totally forgotten about him.* But a snore suggested to him that the man had slept through Dr. Pfeiffer's visit. *Why should I care anyway?* he thought. *Mr. Wrestling Man.*

Maybe Susan is right, thought Johnson. *Maybe she's not. She can't explain Gooch, she can't explain Ellen, at least not with any certainty. I need certainty. Can I take the chance that I might hurt Katy and Zoe again? I don't think so.*

I have to protect Katy and Zoe from Bad News Johnson. I have to leave town until I'm sure I've got control over my own dark side. Yes. That's the only way I can be sure.

I have to leave town.

CHAPTER 20

While seated on the sofa in her mother's living room, Zoe multi-tasked. She had opened several textbooks and was studying amnesia for any clue to her father's condition. She was listening to rain lashing the picture window during a thunderstorm. She was smoking a joint. She was worrying whether air fresheners would be able to erase any evidence of said marijuana before her mother came home. Since school didn't let out until three o'clock and it was now only ten thirty, she gauged her chances as good.

Zoe hadn't smoked in a long time. Her meeting with her father at the hospital, however, had unsettled her. He had changed, whether through regression to age twenty-one or some other psychological mechanism. Any thought that he might have been putting on an act struck her as folly. She intended to help him, and to encourage him not to allow any recovered memories to transform him back to the boor she had known all her life.

Snuffing out her cigarette, she sank back into the cushions. The textbooks offered no assistance.

Another idea occurred to her. It sounded marvelous! She dug out her baby-blue cell from her purse, flipped it open, and punched in the numbers of the Redrock Elementary School main office. But upon dialing the number, she received a harsh beep in her ear, and looked at a readout that said, "No Service." She sighed. Her mother's el cheapo plan seemed to provide no service unless both parties were standing six feet apart atop Stone Mountain.

She recalled that this had happened to her before in the living room. When she moved to the kitchen, the call went through.

"Hi, Mom. Sorry to interrupt you. I know you've been wicked busy up there this week."

"No problem. It's calmed down quite a bit. It's more like an average first week of school now. Most of the grief counselors are still here, but frankly, they've been working with teachers as much as with students today."

After a few minutes of pleading, she persuaded her mother to have lunch with both her and her father.

"Honey," Katy had said, "your dad's state of mind is fragile right now. We're not going to know what to expect."

"What do you mean, 'fragile'? He has amnesia. Other than that, he's very sweet."

"He's never been out here to the school. I just think—"

"Never? In all these years? Why not?"

"I didn't want him here. He was a beast, Zoe. You know that."

"Okay. That was then. Now he's different. He's so kind—"

"Unless his memories come back. Dr. Pfeiffer said that a powerful emotional stimulus could break the amnesia. For all we know, that might be like opening Pandora's box."

"Mom. C'mon! How likely is that to happen?"

"Zoe, my friends' impression of your father is that he's an ogre. That's based on the things I've told them over the years. Most of them don't know about this new and improved version. And those I've tried to explain his amnesia to don't buy it. Their attitude toward him is bound to be hostile. I'd just prefer to play it safe for a while. I want the three of us to get together, I really do, but I think it should happen under more controlled circumstances."

"Such as in a doctor's office."

"Yes."

"Mom, I don't know when that might be possible. I have to go back to school pretty soon. Please. Let's give this a try. I'll call him, I'll pick him up, and drive him to the school."

Katy had reluctantly agreed.

Now it was Zoe who was having second thoughts. While smoking marijuana or drinking wine, her ideas always sounded so fantastic. Later, her sobriety induced doubt. The two problems raised by her mother made sense. First, his memory could come avalanching back at any time, and who knew what his emotional reaction would be? Second, even if that didn't happen, how uncomfortable would he feel walking into a hostile environment?

Remaining in the kitchen, and resisting the impulse to smoke another joint, she dialed her father's number at the hospital.

Johnson had packed, and was ready to go. He had originally planned to call Zoe or Katy to take him home from the hospital, but his decision the night before had changed all that. Now he planned to call a cab. Go home, have the cab wait, throw some clothes and toiletries into his duffel bag, and direct the driver to the Greyhound bus station. He'd sneak out of town, destination unknown. *If you yourself don't know where you're going, how can anyone find you?*

Then Zoe called.

"Dad? Hi."

"Hi, sweetheart."

"Are you still being discharged this morning?"

"Yeah. I'm packing my stuff right now."

"Did you call Mom to pick you up?"

"No… no, I didn't. She's at school, you know."

"Why didn't you call me?"

"I… *um*… was just getting ready to call you, hon. Guess I shouldn't have waited till the last minute. Are you busy? I can take a cab. That won't be a problem."

"No, silly, I'm calling because I want to come and get you. Mom's invited us both to have lunch with her at the school."

"She invited me too?"

"That's, *um*, what she said."

"You're sure she said that she wanted me to come."

"Yes."

Okay, so she was torturing the truth until it screamed for mercy, but he probably would never know. And even if he found out, he'd already be there. She feared that if she didn't say that her mother had extended the invitation, he might not agree to come. After all, the thought of entering the school grounds might jog his recollection that Katy had never before invited him to the school. On the contrary, she had barred him from coming.

As they rode to the school, conversation again came with great difficulty. Trying to make the situation less awkward, Zoe turned on the radio to a pop station and turned up the volume.

"What is that?" asked Johnson.

"They call it rap music," she replied with a small smile. This could be fun. Her father was a tabula rasa now. She could clue him in on current events, current fashions, the whole gamut of modern culture. Like molding a pile of clay into a sculpture, she could use her influence to take Johnson's now young mind and shape it into a totally new version of the man he had previously become.

"But it's not music. It doesn't have a tune."

Zoe sought a frame of reference that might help him appreciate this music. She had seen beatniks in old movies. These bearded, sloppily dressed would-be poets who hung around coffee houses in the fifties. Some guy gave a drum one or two pops while one of the beatniks, who took himself altogether too seriously, recited lines that everyone pretended to understand but no one did. She guessed that reference wouldn't help.

"Nobody in your generation likes it."

For the remainder of the drive, there was little more conversation. Zoe puzzled over the problem of treating this man like a father when he could not remember her as a child. She worried about how he would react if all those years came flooding back. How would he feel? Would he still feel guilty toward Zoe and Katy about anything? All those years waiting behind closed doors, waiting to burst out like the French revolutionaries on Bastille Day. What if he wouldn't believe that he had anything to feel guilty about?

CHAPTER 21

By eleven o'clock, Katy's attempts to concentrate on her work were proving futile. She decided to wait for Johnson and Zoe in the cafeteria, where she could hug and wave at the first kids to enter the cafeteria, second and third graders whom she had known as kindergartners and first graders, until her family showed up. Whenever she entered the cafeteria, hands waved and arms stretched out in hopes of hugs. From all corners came shouts of, "Ms. Nguyen! Ms. Nguyen!"

On her way she stopped by the main office, where all visitors had to register and slap on a big, round, yellow sticker. She asked the secretary, Mrs. Raulston, to let her own visitors know where she would be waiting.

At about noon Johnson and Zoe approached the table, which was as far from the entrance as it was from the faculty table. Even the way Johnson walked, his body language conveyed a personality from Katy's distant past. After a telephone chat with Susan Pfeiffer on Monday, when Katy had asked about Johnson's tests, she had vowed to view Johnson as the young man in his mind, the ever-jovial rake and playmate with the winning smile and the losing arm.

Gray skies had replaced the sunshine, and rain spattered on the cafeteria windows, blowing almost sideways instead of up to down. Lightning flashed and thunder boomed like a giant bass drum. Then followed a long crack of thunder like a building being rent apart followed by another crashing boom.

Katy, surprised, turned to look. "Was it doing this when you came in?"

"No," said Zoe, "but the sky looked something fierce."

Quarter-sized hail began to fall, and piled up on the lawn, leaving many of the kids wide-eyed with wonder and some of them shrieking with fear. The cafeteria was loud, so loud that the din, added to that of the storm, prohibited many from hearing the principal on the PA system. She was asking the teachers to keep checking their e-mail because of a weather situation.

A lithe woman with a long, black ponytail entered the cafeteria. It was Angelina DeLillo, one of Redrock's two assistant principals. She walked casually among the tables as she smiled and returned waves from the kids, and spoke softly to the faculty members who were there. Katy, putting her hand on Zoe's arm, directed her attention to the sudden migration of students out of the cafeteria. Something was wrong. The lunch schedules were staggered. Never should all the kids depart at once, especially when there were no kids coming in to take their places.

"What's happening?" asked Zoe.

"I'm not certain, but it may have to do with the storm."

"Katy," said Johnson. "There's something I need to talk about."

Katy placed her napkin on the table, and rose from her seat. "I need to find out what's going on." Tameka, however, who was turning around a column of her first grade students just as they were entering, waved Katy back as though the situation didn't require Katy to interrupt her family gathering.

Johnson forged on. "Dr. Pfeiffer said my memory could come back any time. No telling when, but it's almost sure to happen. And when it happens, I'm worried that I could change back into the person that you both hate. That's why—that's why I've got to get away."

Preoccupied as she was, those last two words registered on Katy. "What do you mean, 'get away'?"

Johnson looked down at his intertwined fingers. "After lunch, I'm going to get a taxicab to the bus station. Then I'll buy a ticket. I don't even know to where. I don't care. Just far away from here. I won't come back until—unless—I can figure things out."

"Do you really think that's necessary?" asked the ever-reasoning Katy.

"Yes."

"Mind made up, huh?"

"Yes."

"You mean you might not ever come back?" asked Zoe, her eyes covered by a watery glaze.

"I hope I'll be back, Zoe. But the father you've known all your life—Bad News Johnson—he isn't coming back. Ever. I won't let him. I can't. I swear I won't."

By now Katy could barely hear him over the clamor of mass confusion. Teachers sought to line up their classes, first to turn in their trays, then to leave for their classrooms, and sought to accomplish this feat in spatial areas not designed to handle multiple lines of kids. Thus, the lines bunched together with results that were predictable whenever children were squeezed together. Some kids pushed, others tattled, others moved to different spots in line, others cut ahead in line, others whined, "Don't! Stop!" to try to get the teacher's attention.

"Tell you what, pardner," said Katy. "Doesn't look like anybody's going anywhere for a while here. We need to get to the office and find out what's happening." With that she rose and headed for the door, followed by her trembling, weepy daughter and by her ex-husband.

Their journey, however, was no easier than trying to locate a route through a jungle. Children swarmed while teachers barked orders to herd them toward their classrooms. Once there, they would line them up against a hallway wall and have them assume, or in the case of the kindergartners, attempt to teach them, the turtle-like position in which their heads were down at the juncture of the wall and the floor, and their legs were drawn up to their abdomens. Keeping the youngest ones in that position for more than two minutes was as impossible as forcing a cat to lie still while you fed her a pill. Their teachers had to be as vigilant as Intensive Care nurses as so many kids wriggled uncomfortably. Some children broke out in tears, some cried loudly, having soaked up the fear that the teachers were experiencing, just as the little human sponges typically internalized the emotions that adults modeled, even when the adults preferred not to model such emotions.

The three of them neared the cafeteria door. The storm sounded as though it were abating, at least enough so that Katy could hear Mrs. Drummond's voice over the PA system. "I need everyone's attention. We now have a tornado warning. The tornado may well miss us, but we cannot take that chance. What we want here is to get the older students, as many as possible, into the gymnasium, and into the position that they have been taught during all our drills. We are already putting the remaining students in the hallways in the same position. Please do your best to make this process as orderly as possible. Thank you."

Katy had heard Mrs. Drummond's announcement through all the commotion leading from the cafeteria, but she didn't know what to do with her family. Zoe watched her as if expecting instructions. Johnson looked dazed and confused. "What can I do?" he asked.

"I don't know yet."

She was about to enter the office for confirmation that she had heard all the salient details correctly when Angelina took her by the elbow. "Viv and Sandy are heading for the gym. Let's you and I troll the hallways to see if any teachers need help."

Angelina peered over Katy's shoulder, noticing Zoe and her father. "Is this your family?" she asked.

"Yes," replied Katy. "Meet my daughter Zoe and my ex-husband. Zoe, Johnson, this is Angelina DeLillo, one of our assistant principals." She knew that the timing of this family reunion couldn't have been worse if it were taking place during a nuclear holocaust. To lift the veil of worry from Angelina's face, she added, "They can help us with the kids."

"Good," said Angelina. "That's good. We can use all the help we can get."

While Katy and Zoe wandered the halls, Johnson stood at the front double glass doors and stared out at the storm. They all could hear the cries of panicked or restless children, the splashing of raindrops falling onto the aluminum cover that extended from the school lobby out over the concrete walkway that separated the front doors from the street where the buses parked, and larger drops of rain tumbling heavily from the awning onto the walkway.

It was dark as night. One might have thought a solar eclipse was taking place. The rain fell, heavy but in thinner drops, waving in the wind like a wheat field in Nebraska. At that moment came a flash of lightning that felt to Katy like someone using a camera flash device inches from her eyes. The report of thunder that followed could have been a cord of giant redwood trees dropped from hundreds of feet in the air.

The power went out at Redrock Elementary. As far as Katy was concerned, she felt fortunate that the power had lasted this long, such was the ferocity of the storm. The kids reacted differently. She could hear screams from the suddenly dark corridors.

Then she heard another sound. This was the one she had dreaded. It was the deep, chugging sound of a freight train. Anyone who had listened to the reports of tornado survivors knew what it meant. She joined Johnson at the door and looked at the southern sky to confirm the worst. From the black clouds overhead dropped a wide funnel, growing larger and larger by the second, close enough that she could see debris spinning around inside the dark-gray, twisting monster that approached the school, lurching left and right, but not sufficiently to deviate from its course. She stood there stock-still, marveling at the swirling contents, which might have been furniture or metal signs or parts of vehicles or limbs of trees. Or people. The tornado occupied half of the visible sky.

Katy could see that the entire staff was distraught. Trying to keep the kids, especially the kindergartners and first graders, in that awkward position against the walls while undoubtedly sensing what was coming could whiten the hair of a thirty-year-old. She noticed that now both Johnson and Zoe were standing on the sidewalk, gazing at the funnel as though they were merely watching some documentary on television. Katy had to yank them both inside by their elbows.

The adults waited until the last possible moment to join the children on the floor. They had to be certain that none of the children were stirring, no minor feat since virtually all of the kids were crying and screaming out of sheer terror. Inside the school, as far as Katy could see, a blackness so deep as to give the impression of outer space cast its titanic shadow over humanity as well as walls, ceilings, and hallways. Katy and Zoe pulled Johnson down, each holding an arm.

Redrock Elementary's building proved no match for this disaster. Katy could hear the tornado peel off the steel roof as if opening the pop-top on a can of soda. She knew that that would expose cables and water pipes to the storm's fury, and that the violent wind would snap both. Sure enough, water cascaded down onto her and the others. The water felt cold, sending a chill down her spine. She had always thought that the ceiling tiles seemed to be scant more than pasteboard. The weight of the water had obviously caused the ceilings to cave in. Fragments of fluorescent lights pinched her back. She heard a sound that could only have been falling bricks from the corridor walls.

The noises made by the twisting metal roof and exploding windows were horrific. Papers and debris flew out of classrooms.

And then it was over.

CHAPTER 22

Screams of children and adults alike pierced the air. Smells of dust and blood and musky water-soaked carpets filled what remained of the hallways. Some of the dust turned out to be black smoke emanating from the cafeteria. A fire-breathing dragon sent fingers of flame creeping out of the kitchen. The tornado had struck at the height of lunchtime. It appeared that cheap, budget-saving, wiring had sparked a flame when the winds had tossed kitchen appliances hither and fro.

Johnson heard the screams, smelled the odors, and dove in to help cafeteria workers put out the fire. He had seen many of the staff and children run outside the building to safety, but he had also seen many children retreat in panic farther down the darkened corridors. When he was satisfied that they had subdued the fire, he took off after those children. Running was difficult. Ever since he had awoken on I-85 that fateful afternoon, both his knees, but especially his right knee, had objected to rapid movement. Even limping fast caused considerable pain.

The winds carried the sound of sirens from north, south, east, and west. Ambulances were doubtlessly on their way here, there, and everywhere in the county. Within a few minutes Johnson would hear helicopters overhead. They would be the first emergency responders to arrive. So many streets were impassable due to storm damage, debris, and power outages. It didn't help that Redrock Elementary sat atop a hill with only one narrow road leading to and from the highway below. Teachers, bloodied and bruised, carrying children in their arms, were hustling kids outside into what was now a steady downpour.

Many of the children limped, most were crying, some in the teachers' arms were unconscious. Clothes hung ripped and bloodstained, some faces partially covered by rivers of blood, and drenched by the water flowing down from the ceiling out of the busted pipes. Patches of pink insulation material, undoubtedly containing asbestos, stuck in hair, on arms, and on clothing.

Johnson moved deeper into the bowels of the carnage, moving bricks frantically, searching for children, whom he pulled out delicately, then passed to the arms of a teacher. While tossing bricks from one pile, another portion of the wall collapsed on him. The corner of a brick cut a gash in the back of his head. He thought another brick may have struck him in the middle of his back.

Awakening from a daze to find himself sitting against the opposite wall, he touched the spot that burned on his head and studied the blood on his hand as though he were examining nothing more personal than a slide under a microscope. His back and left side hurt also, perhaps from broken ribs. All his painful joints rebelled from movement. He could barely move his fingers. He was shivering, the result of scurrying through a waterfall earlier. Still, he thought, this is mid-August, and it's not like they've got the A/C turned on. Fever? He felt his forehead, and it felt warmer than a heating pad. *Never min*d, he thought as he resumed digging. *I'll just have to get used to it.*

After handing off a child, he would scramble toward the direction of more children's cries. He heard a whimper, and now he saw a bright yellow T-shirt. Sneezing from the dust, he carefully carried out the boy, whose T-shirt bore a picture of a gang of superheroes. Johnson hoped they were superheroes. Each wore a snarling grin and held futuristic weapons. Shaking badly, his face tear-stained and dust-stained, more teeth missing than present, the boy asked, "Did my house fall down, too?"

"Can you walk?" asked Johnson, ignoring the question that he couldn't provide a comforting response to.

"I can't. My leg hurts. I think it's broke."

Johnson hoisted him up. "That's okay, fella. We're gonna fix that leg good as new." He looked around for someone to take the child but could locate no one. He wondered whether everyone else had already left. Could that be possible? Surely not. It was just so dark in here, and quiet because everyone had to watch their step.

He trotted carefully to the school's front doors and laid the kid down at the entrance. The boy started crying loudly, the nature of his predicament having finally hit him like one of the school's brick walls. Johnson hated to leave him like that, but he knew someone would come to the child's assistance immediately. Meanwhile, he had more work to do, and he didn't want anything other than his own aches and pains slowing him down. Head throbbing, he hobbled back inside.

Johnson marveled at the extent to which the corridors of the school had turned into black caves. The environs were like a night without moon or stars. He walked around the circular office, sometimes having to put a hand out to prevent slamming into walls, searching for the next sign of a child in need. Had the roof buckled over the office, that would have provided some light. But of course, that also would have meant further weakening of the structure and greater likelihood of injuries.

Thus far most of the children he had discovered had been far down the corridors. Who knew how they had gotten to such inaccessible places? Most likely they had panicked and run as far as they could when the tornado hit. *What idiot designed this place?* Johnson wondered. It resembled a wheel with the administrative offices in the middle and corridors leading like spokes out to a distant hallway that encircled the school like Interstate 285 encircled Atlanta. Thus, moving among adjacent corridors meant going back to the office or out to the perimeter hallway.

At the mouth of a corridor opposite the front doors, he almost bumped into a tall, thin woman whose long black hair was wet and stringy.

"Zoe! What are you doing here?"

"I saw you put a little boy down at the front door, and I ran in. I want to help."

"Well, you've got to get out of here. Go help your mom outside. It's dangerous back here."

"Where you go, I go."

"And her mom's not outside," said Katy from behind him.

"Have you two—"

"Deal with it," said Katy.

"You're a counselor," said Johnson. "Shouldn't you be outside helping with all those kids?"

"Sandy can help outside. Zoe and I are going to help you."

Zoe touched his arm. "Listen! I hear a little girl crying. Over there!" She pointed down the passageway.

They located the girl, sitting with legs outstretched just inside a classroom, crying loudly. As Zoe swept her up into her arms, the child said, "Mommy'll be mad because I ruined my new dress!" Johnson noticed a small pond of blood above her right ear. Mud and blood smeared her bright red dress.

"Okay, Zoe," he said. "You take care of her. Katy, you go with her while I—"

"Not a chance, cowboy," replied Katy, grabbing his hand. "We all stay together. I don't intend to lose either of you inside this dark hell."

Johnson silently acquiesced. If they were determined to share this crumbling building with him, he would rather they stay close by so that he could keep an eye on them.

Katy carried the little girl to the front door since the child knew her. Johnson and Zoe stayed back in the shadows listening keenly for cries, screams, or shouts while

Katy hugged the child and talked to her. She patted her on the back, and the girl ran outside.

"Have you always been this stubborn?" Johnson asked Zoe.

"You'll have to get your memory back to find out," she replied.

"Where are the police or firemen or whatever?"

"Having a tough time," replied Katy. "The whole county's a mess. Mrs. Drummond told me that some emergency people are trying to get here by helicopter. And most of our teachers, along with Sandy, you haven't met her, she's our other counselor, are outside trying to settle the kids down. We had half a dozen or so make a jailbreak toward the highway. Took four teachers to round them all up."

"Bottom line," observed Johnson. "We're going to have to get as many kids as we can as fast as we can. Doesn't sound like we have a lot of help back here."

"Nobody has a lot of help."

The three of them began to slink down another black hallway, backs against the wall. Before they had gone far, a chubby girl with all of her upper front baby teeth missing called out, "Ms. Nguyen! Ms. Nguyen!"

"Carmen! Why aren't you outside?"

"I was scared."

"Well, get going! Hurry!"

"My bus went away without me!" she cried. She had a sign around her neck in the shape and color of a yellow school bus, with the number four scrawled in large black letters by a Sharpie. "I'm s'posed to be on number four, but it went already, and it didn't take me!"

Katy kissed her on the cheek. "It'll be okay, sweetie. No buses have gone anywhere. We'll get you home, I promise. Go on now." After Carmen had scrambled away, she said, "Where do they get these ideas? Buses?!" Perhaps the child had mistaken the sound of helicopters for buses.

Together they explored another corridor. This time they all heard crying. It emanated from a classroom that fallen bricks partially blocked. Johnson began to move them, but Zoe tossed them aside much faster. *The joy of no arthritis,* thought Johnson.

Inside the classroom they came upon a black girl with dark-rimmed glasses who was crying loudly. Her glasses hung awkwardly, as though one stem had been broken. Johnson noticed blood on them, and motioned to Katy, who dropped to one knee, and stroked her back.

"I can't find Mejia!" she cried. "Mommy told me to take care of Mejia, and I can't find her!"

"Honey, your head is bleeding. We'll look for your sister, but we need to take you up to where the doctors are."

Johnson was beginning to appreciate the value of having Katy around. Since so many of the children knew her, she was able to comfort them on the spot. Katy aimed the child for the exit, where a teacher quickly intercepted her.

Hearing screams, they raced down another corridor, Johnson relying on the strength of his daughter and ex-wife, as he had to lean on them occasionally for balance and mobility.

"There's someone down here!" said Zoe, running ahead of them.

"Zoe, be care—" began Katy, but she was too late. Zoe tripped over a brick and went sprawling, bracing her fall with her elbows. When she sat up, blood drooled from her left elbow.

"We'll have to get you to one of the EMTs," said Johnson.

"No. I'm okay. It's just a scratch. Listen. It's coming from that classroom." She pointed to a door just opposite them.

The room was so full of dust that they all coughed harshly. Advancing on a mountain of overturned tables and chairs, they heard the sobs. Johnson, without much help from Zoe this time, and feeling a surge of adrenaline, tossed them aside as if they were foam rubber. Underneath the furniture a girl was lying in the fetal position, quiet now, a thumb in her mouth, her black hair tied into two ponytails, her white T-shirt, emblazoned with the words "Sweet lil' brat" in pink, that she was yet to grow into, extending past her knees. He gently felt her body to see whether this cursory examination produced any wails of pain. It didn't. The child said nothing as he took her into his arms. He was in the hallway when she wriggled and protested.

"My book bag!" she cried. "I got a new Hannah Montana book bag!" She was struggling to break free.

"I'll look for it," said Zoe.

"No," said Katy. "I'll buy her another book bag. We have to get out of here."

From the vantage point of the hallway, they could see ceiling tiles in the classroom sagging from water pressure.

Curtains of water, like plastic shower curtains, fell from the sides of several tiles, and the tortured metal roof continued to creak and shift, forcing computer and TV cables downward.

Katy's fears about the classroom were soon validated. They had taken no more than three steps into the hall when most of the ceiling came crashing down, blowing dust and splinters out the door as if the giant storm were wheezing with its final breaths. The girl didn't cry; she just stuck her thumb back into her mouth. Johnson carried her to the front of the office, set her down, and whispered into her ear, "Run!"

She took off, but looked back when she reached the glass doors. Her expression was not fear, but innocent surprise.

"Hurry!" she called to him.

He waved at her. "We'll be there in a minute! You go now!"

Another child's cry guided them down another dark corridor, where they faced new challenges. Zoe continued to hold her left arm awkwardly.

"I don't like the looks of that," noted Johnson.

"I'm fine," replied Zoe, looking away, hiding her watery eyes.

To enter this classroom, they had to push with all their might because the teacher's desk had been blown against the other side of the door. It seemed to take an hour, but Johnson knew it had actually required a few minutes of time and an hour's worth of strength. Finally they each squeezed through.

"Help me?" said a shivering voice underneath the desk. "I need help."

It was a boy wearing a white T-shirt depicting a T-Rex dinosaur over navy shorts. His brown hair was unkempt, but Johnson had a feeling that it had been so when he had gotten off the bus this morning. He knelt down, causing a twinge like a knife in his mid-back and a shallow coughing spasm that he couldn't stop. He had to wait until the cough had run its course, like a garbage-can top dropped on the sidewalk, rattling until it gradually settled to a peaceful stop. He ignored the looks this drew from Katy and Zoe.

"Hey there, friend," Johnson said weakly. As he extended his hand toward the boy, who was cowering as far away from him as possible in the well of the desk, his back and side complained fiercely. "Come with me."

"Miss Lattimore said I could take my pitcher home to my daddy. Can you go get it?"

There was no time. Johnson knew this.

"Ms. Nguyen!" shouted the boy, extending his arms.

Johnson observed the clutter of overturned chairs and tables, paper, crayons, and markers all over the floor, and a lamp and boom box smashed to pieces. "It was over there," the boy cried, dragging Katy to a nondescript pile of mess that could have been deposited by a garbage truck.

"Son," said Johnson. "We have to leave. It's dangerous in here."

But after sorting through several drawings in madcap fashion, the boy said, "Here it is!" He showed it to her triumphantly. "Do you like it?"

His speech pattern reminded Johnson of Ellen. "Here" came out "he-oo."

The picture was on white construction paper. In black were two stick figures, one larger than the other, both smiling. What appeared to be a dog was also smiling. A house was colored red with two windows above a brown door. Purple smoke swirled from a chimney. At the bottom was a line of green for the grass, and at the top was a similar line of blue for the sky. In the upper left corner was a smiling yellow circle. Katy commented on each of these details while carrying the child out of the classroom. "You worked so hard on this. Your dad's gonna love it," she said.

"Is Rufus okay? Did he get hurt?"

"Who is Rufus, son?" asked Johnson.

"He's my dog! There in the pitcher!"

A kid could put you in a corner faster than a Harvard lawyer. What should he do, lie? Then face the prospect that the kid would be hurt worse than ever if his dog had actually been harmed? No way. "Tell you what. I really don't know. Ask those nice people outside if they can find out for you, okay?" As they neared the entrance, Johnson, Katy, and Zoe remained behind in the shadows.

"Ain't you comin'?" asked the boy.

"We have to stay in here," said Johnson. "You go find your dad. Those men will help you." Johnson was looking at EMTs who had finally made it to the school and were running toward the entrance.

"Okay, mister," the boy said. He ran to the door.

When they were certain that the child was in safe hands, they returned to the dark, creaking, rumbling, splashing hallways, like navigating the sewers underneath an old city.

CHAPTER 23

They were exploring their darkest corridor yet. But this was the direction from which they had all heard crying.

Johnson and Katy kept asking, and Zoe kept reassuring, that she was all right. He worried, however, about the way she was favoring her left elbow.

The exact classroom was dimly lit by streaks of sunlight against the windows. Since they were on the east side of the building, the sun provided little more than an outline of their greatest challenge thus far.

Two twin girls were cringing together, arms around each other, in the remains of a bookshelf. This wooden apparatus was holding up the closed circuit television. About thirty books had not fallen yet, but every few seconds one or two came tumbling down. Every book that fell to the floor further destabilized the bookshelf, and if it came down, the TV would come crashing down on top of it. Removing the children from the shelf where they huddled would also subtract enough weight to initiate the deadly chain reaction.

As Johnson neared the girls, walking softly, he could see their eyes, which appeared red from crying, widen. They spoke a few words to him, but not in English.

"What language is that?" asked Johnson as he tried to size up the obstacles.

"It's an Asian language," said Katy. "Sounds Korean."

"They're so cute!" said Zoe.

"How are we going to do this?" asked Katy.

"I don't know," said Johnson. "This one's tricky. One false move, and those kids won't have a chance." He turned to Katy and Zoe. "I need you two to go to the front and get help. I'll stay here and watch the situation."

"Why both of us?" asked Katy. "Why not just Zoe?"

"Why me?" asked Zoe.

"Zoe, they may not let you come back," said Johnson. "I think you may have broken your elbow. And we need to have someone who can lead them back here, not just give directions."

Katy kissed his cheek. "Okay. Be careful." She also wanted Zoe's elbow attended to.

"Hurry."

After they were gone, he stood studying the problem. He heard the groaning sound of stress being applied to boards. He breathed deeply, feeling his ribs rattle as he did. If necessary, he would have to act fast. Could he in his weakened condition? But he would entertain no questions. There were kids to save.

Half a dozen books tumbled to the floor. The children, shrieking, slid to the opposite end of the shelf. *I've got to act now,* he thought.